NANCY WARREN

GAME OF THORNS

VILLAGE FLOWER SHOP
COZY MYSTERY - BOOK 5

Ambleside Publishing

Introduction

ROSES ARE BEAUTIFUL BUT BEWARE THE
THORNS...

When eight strangers turn up at a beautiful hotel in the
Cotswolds in England for a weekend of flower arranging,
they're thinking of making their own arrangements for
dinner parties, gifts and even weddings. But even as the rose's
blooms hide its sharp thorns, so the relaxing weekend hides
dark forces. Jealousy, fear, and hatred lurk beneath the
surface.

Peony Bellefleur, who owns Bewitching Blooms in the
picture-postcard pretty village of Willow Waters is teaching
the flower arranging classes. Peony's a witch and this
weekend coincides with the full moon. She'll be gathering
with her coven for a full moon ceremony while the myste-
rious and gorgeous Lord Fitzlupin, aka Alex her werewolf
boyfriend, gets locked into his dungeon until the full moon
passes.

Peony's looking forward to a weekend sharing her love of

flowers when murder enters the arrangement. Can she solve the crime before the killer strikes again?

Come join me and my unusual friends in my latest adventure.

"A modern-day Agatha Christie. This mystery was as smooth as a Swiss watch and as cozy as a café au lait with a chocolate croissant." *****

And if you haven't met Rafe Crosyer yet, he's the gorgeous, sexy vampire in *The Vampire Knitting Club* series. You can get his origin story free when you join Nancy's no-spam newsletter at NancyWarrenAuthor.com.

Come join Nancy in her private Facebook group where we talk about books, knitting, pets, and life.
www.facebook.com/groups/NancyWarrenKnitwits

GAME OF THORNS

Chapter One

There's something about early September that I've always loved. Not quite summer, not quite fall, the sun is golden but the air is crisp and the leaves are beginning to turn. I like knowing that soon the trees will show off their full range: burnt orange, pale yellow, and deep, flaming reds. Okay, my adopted home of Willow Waters in the heart of the Cotswolds in England doesn't display the glories of a New England autumn, but I've come to love my village in all its seasons.

No doubt some of my current happiness was due to the new man in my life, Alex Stanford, aka Lord Fitzlupin, who was currently driving us in his dark green Jaguar to another Cotswold village to have Sunday lunch. We liked to get out of Willow Waters for our dates because no one (apart from my mom, Jessie Rae, and two housemates, Char and Hilary) knew that we were romantically involved. A lot of gossip takes place in small villages and Alex and I had very strong reasons not to draw attention to ourselves. After all, it's not every day that a witch and a werewolf start dating. So, let's just say we had enough on our plates without the rest of Willow Waters getting involved.

We passed Barnham House, where the archeological dig for recently-discovered Roman ruins was still taking place. It had been a couple of weeks since I was up this way, and I was surprised to see how much earth they'd excavated.

I said to Alex, "I'm all for wanting to understand our history, but it does seem an awful shame to disrupt the land this way. They must be unsettling the trees, not to mention uprooting some of the garden's more gorgeous blooms." As the owner of Bewitching Blooms, Willow Waters' flower shop, I was always thinking about the soil and the natural world. I was protective of all flowers, even the ones I wasn't buying for the store.

Alex nodded, glancing for a moment at the site, a serious expression on his face. "That garden is a good reminder that you never know what's beneath the land you're standing on. Barnham House was famous for its outstanding grounds—but like much of the British Isles, when you dig below the surface, you never know what you'll find. For much of history we've built over what's gone before us." I knew that was true, and it was exciting having a TV show made about the archeological find right in our own neighborhood.

Alex paused and I could tell something was on his mind. I waited, knowing him well enough now to sense when he needed time to find the right words.

"I wanted some time alone with you now as it's a full moon this coming weekend," he said.

Softly, I replied, "I know." Alex couldn't control the strength of his powers on a full moon and relied on his trusty butler, George, to lock him in the dungeon of Fitzlupin Castle for the duration.

"I never used to mind being locked away over those few days but now I hate the idea that I couldn't come to you if you needed me," he said.

"It's okay," I told him, sensing how difficult it was for him to talk about these things. Apart from his trusted butler, Alex had kept his true identity a secret for all his forty years. I knew it must be hard for him to be open with me. But I appreciated it. I said, "When you have to 'go away' for the weekend, I miss you."

Alex took his eyes off the road just long enough to flash me a warm smile. I laid a hand on his knee, something I loved to do while he was driving. Alex was objectively the most handsome man in Willow Waters, and his profile was exceptional. A strong jawline, elegant nose, and a thick head of near-black hair with a few streaks of pure silver. I had a particular fondness for the faint wrinkles at the corner of his blue-gray eyes. Wolf's eyes.

Snapping back to reality I said, "Besides, I'm going to be kept busy teaching flower arranging at the Tudor Rose this weekend. They asked me to focus on roses, which makes sense, of course, but it isn't as easy as it sounds for beginners."

I thought this might have set his mind at rest, but he still looked a little worried as he said, "I'm glad you'll be occupied."

I grinned. "You do remember that I have some pretty strong powers of my own? Plus, an entire coven of sisters to call on if something goes wrong?" I tried to imagine what could possibly go awry at a flower-arranging event in a beautiful hotel. "I'm sure there'll be nothing more serious happening this weekend than a few pricked thumbs. A broken vase at worst." Not exactly the kind of stuff that would warrant a werewolf to the rescue.

I looked back at Alex. There was a small smile at his lips but his brow was still furrowed. I wanted to reassure him further but I had the feeling it wouldn't matter what I said. He wanted to protect me, which was unnecessary, but still kind of heartwarming.

I squeezed his knee again and then turned to the window to watch the village disappear behind us. Willow Waters had been my home for six years, but I'd been too focused on the business and renovating my farmhouse to really explore the beauty of the Cotswolds. Alex, on the other hand, seemed to know just about every cozy pub and tavern, and every charming restaurant and scenic spot in the region. For a man who had a reputation as something of a recluse, I'd been pleasantly surprised to discover this side of him. Unable to hold back my curiosity, I'd asked him about it once and he explained that his late parents had been social creatures. And for business purposes (Alex imported fine wines) he had to know the good spots to host clients—and find new ones.

I wound down the window and let the crisp air whip back my hair. I'd worn it down, with a denim dress, and a green cardigan to keep me warm. Lush trees and swathes of green hills rushed past in a pretty vista until a village of thatched cottages rose up ahead.

"Welcome to Kingham Village," Alex said. "One of my favorite places in the Cotswolds."

After a few minutes, he pulled up outside a gorgeous pub called The Orange Tree. He stepped out of the Jag and came to my side to open the door. I loved his old-school sense of chivalry, even though I could have opened that door myself without lifting a finger. I took his hand and we walked through the door into the bar. At one end, a log fire was flickering, a few patrons drinking ales relaxing in leather armchairs around it. It was warm and cozy, with exposed brick and wooden floorboards, soft yellow lights illuminating the corners. The pub was already busy, the sound of laughter and chatter rising above clinking glasses.

Alex had chosen well, as he always did.

The maître d' greeted him warmly and took us to a table in the back dining room of the pub. I inhaled deeply. The mouthwatering scent of slow-cooked meat, a stew maybe, was making me hungry. I smiled as I saw Alex scent the air. As a werewolf, his sense of smell was heightened and I knew he'd be appreciating it even more than me.

Alex pulled out my chair and once I was seated, sat down opposite me. I didn't even try to conceal my happiness. I just adored sharing a good meal with Alex. He was an excellent conversationalist, a connoisseur of all things food and drink, and handsome to boot. If you hadn't already guessed, I'm pretty smitten.

I glanced down at the menu. It was a perfunctory gesture. I knew exactly what I was going to order.

"Two of the beef and ale pies?" Alex asked.

"Absolutely."

He examined the wine list and then ordered two glasses of Burgundy along with a basket of freshly-baked bread, some olives, and our pies. It was our last date for a little while, after all.

With the waiter gone, Alex leaned across the table and

took my hand. "I've been looking forward to this moment all week," he said.

I felt the same and told him so. There was something about having to steal away from Willow Waters which made our time together even more special. Every date felt like a treat. When the waiter brought the starters and the wine, we clinked glasses, and I took a long sip. I looked around the room. There was a nice mix of families, people who were clearly locals, and the inevitable tourists. "This is nice."

"I'm glad you like it." Alex smiled. "I've brought a couple of business clients here and the food has always been great but it's much more fun sharing these places with you."

"Thank you," I said a little shyly. Since Alex always chose his words carefully, I was often a little floored when he paid me compliments. Each one felt like a birthday and Christmas gift all rolled into one. I sat back in my seat and took in the room. And that's when I saw someone who looked familiar. I felt my body tense, desperate to hold on to the privacy of our budding relationship. But as I narrowed my glance, focusing in on the attractive brunette and noticing her sharp cheek-bones and intense expression, I realized the face did not belong to a fellow Willower.

To Alex, I said, "Do you recognize that woman?" I gestured to the corner of the room where a petite woman, who looked to be about thirty with short, stylish brown hair, was deep in conversation with a handsome man who was about the same age and sported a striking mop of reddish-brown curls.

Alex turned his head ever so slightly, always conscious of being discreet.

Turning back to me he shook his head. "I can't say I do. Should I?"

And then it clicked. "It's Tamsin Mortimer. That's who it is. She was a ranked tennis player, retired now, but the last I heard she was on the latest season of British Ballroom. I saw a few of the episodes. She was an incredible dancer."

I paused at Alex's confused expression. I'd become as hooked as half of Britain on British Ballroom, the show that paired professional dancers with celebrities from other walks of life. It was great fun watching a famous comedian do the tango or a soap star kick up her heels in a foxtrot. Of course, Alex had no idea who Tamsin Mortimer was—the man had zero interest in popular shows and didn't even own a TV. I'd lost count of the times I'd started a sentence with, *Did you ever watch...?* before remembering that the answer was always *No.*

"Ah," he said, a little bemused. "Right, then."

"Well, she was in all the papers for a while because she left the show early."

"Is that one of those reality shows where they get voted off?"

"Yes." At least he knew the basics. "But during filming she developed an obsessive fan who was then arrested for stalking. After she was off the show, she disappeared from the limelight. It was rumored that she'd moved with her husband to a small fishing village in Argentina." I looked again at the table. Tamsin's complexion was as creamy as a glass of whole milk. "Though she probably holed up somewhere much closer to home."

"What a horrible thing to go through." He shuddered, and I knew a wave of deep empathy was coursing through his body. "Honestly, I don't understand the cult of celebrity at all. We should just allow talented people who just happen to be in the public eye to live their lives as normal."

I agreed, and then we paused, both glancing over again at the table. Although the couple weren't touching, I could feel the intensity of their connection across the room. Those two had passion. Even though I didn't know Tamsin Mortimer personally, I was happy she'd obviously moved on from a bad experience.

Then our pies arrived and I forgot all about the former tennis star and dancing contestant as Alex and I fell into a blissful silence as we savored the flakey, buttery pastry and the first bite of succulent slow-cooked filling.

"Perfect," he murmured, and I knew his cultivated taste buds were doing their own special dance—deserving their own spot on British Ballroom.

We slipped into easy conversation about the week, and I told Alex a little more about the upcoming flower-arranging course. "I think there are eight people signed up, which is a good number for our first weekend workshop. If it's successful, I imagine we'll do more."

I was about to go on, when the man who'd been engaged in intense conversation with Tamsin Mortimer suddenly jumped up, left the table, and strode out of the room. I didn't think he'd left to go to the bathroom. Tamsin looked distraught and if it was possible, she turned even paler. Her gaze stayed fixed on where he'd been, and I could tell that she was hoping he would walk back through the door. But the only person to arrive at her table was the waiter, brandishing two plates of what looked to be lemon tart. Pulled back to the present, Tamsin shook her head at the dessert and instead motioned for the bill.

Alex had followed my gaze and as I met his eyes, he shook his head firmly. "I can understand a lovers' quarrel, but no gentleman leaves a woman sitting alone in a restaurant," he informed me. "And he certainly doesn't leave her with the bill."

Old-fashioned he might be, but I was pleased to know he'd never storm out of a restaurant when he was with me, even if we did have a fight.

"I can feel that poor woman's pain," I said. It was coming to me in waves and I couldn't shut it out.

Alex nodded. "She feels distant from the most important person in her life. It's exactly how I feel when I have to lock myself away from you on the full moon." He gripped my hand tighter. "I really meant it when I said I hate knowing I couldn't get to you if you needed me."

I was shocked at how candid Alex was being about his emotions. And then just as quickly, I was overcome by the realization that I wanted to be candid about mine. Alex was fast becoming the most important person in my life. My heart leapt into my throat, and I wasn't sure that I'd be able to find the right words but then I swallowed and said exactly what I needed to. "I feel the same way."

Alex broke into a relieved smile. It would have taken him a lot to put his emotions on the line that way. I was proud of him. I was proud of us!

I tried not to stare as Tamsin Mortimer paid the bill and made a quick exit, her head down so as to avoid eye contact with anyone in the dining room.

Too full for dessert, we asked for our own bill so that we could stroll around the pub's garden.

I took Alex's hand in mine and felt a wave of contentment flood through me. I'd had a delicious meal, with a delicious man, who'd pretty much told me I was at the center of his thoughts. It had been so many years since I'd felt this happy that I wanted to take stock of this moment. To appreciate my luck.

The garden was beautiful, and as I sniffed the late summer roses, I spied a white rose which had fallen from its bush and lay on the ground. I bent down to scoop it up and as I did, I murmured a few words to imbue it with peace and calmness, hoping it would help Alex get through the couple of days when we wouldn't be able to communicate with one another. This was one of the upshots of dating a witch—my power to add positive emotions to flowers, making bouquets which could help the sick heal or the bereaved to feel less sorrowful. Even make the lovesick a little more hopeful.

Smiling, I turned to Alex and reached for the buttonhole on his sports jacket. As I looped the flower through the hole, Alex said, "I'll take this into the dungeon with me at the weekend. It will remind me of you and of this lovely afternoon."

With incredible tenderness, he cupped my face in his hands, and I closed my eyes as his lips found mine. There was nothing so nice as the warmth of Alex's skin against mine.

Even though we'd be parted over duration of the full moon, I had a busy agenda. There was a coven meeting to look forward to, and I'd be sharing my love of flowers and flower arranging with a group of students.

I was looking forward to a calm, happy weekend, where the most that could go wrong would be someone pricking their finger on a rose thorn.

If only.

Chapter Two

I took a moment before entering my shop, Bewitching Blooms, and watched my colleague, Imogen, hard at work. You might think me boastful, but sometimes I still had to pinch myself at what a beautiful business I owned and how lucky I was to employ someone like Imogen. She was a real talent. I dealt with the practical side of the business, but Imogen was a master florist. I knew I would never be as good as she was—I didn't have the same artistic eye, but I was pretty good at creating a more casual look that was an unstructured, unforced profusion of color. At twenty-four, Imogen was driven and hard-working, and since she'd returned to Willow Waters after university in London, she also knew all the locals, which came in handy for a relative newbie like me. What I mean to say is, I trusted her and I respected her and I knew she was a good part of the reason business was currently thriving.

The bell dinged as I entered, and Blue, a marmalade cat and my familiar, briefly lifted her head from where she'd been snoozing in a sunny corner and blinked at me slowly. I gave her a quick stroke, enjoying the feel of her warm fur, and then put down my bags. Imogen called out a hello and then gestured to the bursting buckets of roses that were neatly lined at her feet. "The flowers arrived. It's so much more than I imagined," she said, not unhappily. Imogen liked to be busy. She was talking about the order for the Tudor Rose Inn flower-arranging weekend. On the table were rolls of satiny ribbon in a host of colors, spongy green biodegradable florist's foam, and rolls of tape I'd painstakingly sorted and counted before my romantic lunch. There was a lot to organize and I was glad that Imogen was there to help.

"How's it been over lunch?" I asked, setting down my bag and pulling my hair back into a ponytail, ready to get to work.

"Not too busy," she said, shrugging. "It goes like that sometimes on a Friday lunchtime. The rush is either in the morning or just before we're closing. Anyway, it gave me time to prepare enough of our signature arrangements for the weekend trade, since no one will be here to make anything. It's going to be weird handing the shop over to a stranger while we're at the Tudor Rose."

I laughed. "Char isn't a stranger. She lives with me. And if Roberto at the coffee shop trusts her with his business, we should feel honored he's letting us have her for the weekend. I don't know anyone with higher standards than Roberto."

Imogen laughed and tossed back her glossy blonde ponytail. "You have a point."

Although Char was only a couple of years younger than Imogen, those two were chalk and cheese. Char was into cars and tattoos, Imogen pink nail polish and spa weekends. Also, Char was a witch and Imogen wasn't.

The bell rang out and in walked a beautiful woman and

what I assumed was her equally beautiful mother. Each had a head of tumbling chestnut curls and they held themselves proudly upright. The daughter was dressed in a burgundy shirtdress; the mother wore a silk shirt and tailored trousers. Immediately I knew that they both appreciated the finer things in life and would no doubt be looking for something extra-special from the shop. I greeted them and asked how I could help.

The mother flashed a charming smile and introduced herself as Arabella Ainsworth. "This is my daughter, Verity. We're here this weekend to take your flower-arranging course. Verity is getting married, you see, and I intend to make the bridal bouquet myself."

"What a lovely idea," I said. "There's nothing like the personal touch at a wedding." I was being truthful, although she might have been doing me, or another hard-working florist, out of a potential job. "And we're looking forward to welcoming you tomorrow. This is my colleague, Imogen, who'll be running the course with me."

Arabella nodded and gave Imogen a nod. "We're looking forward to it as well."

Verity had yet to speak and I noted that she looked less than thrilled about her mother's passion project. She probably had ideas of her own about her wedding. I knew what it was like to have something of an overbearing mother, so I flashed her an understanding smile and said, "Congratulations on your engagement."

She thanked me and reflexively touched her ring. It caught the sunlight which was streaming through the window and I caught my breath a little at the stone. It was a whopper of a teardrop diamond set on a band of twinkling baguettes.

Arabella said, "We thought we'd just pop in to make sure the roses will be fresh and varied for the bridal bouquet I intend to practice."

Okay, so she was here for quality control. Overbearing might have been an understatement.

Verity sighed loudly, her frustration with her mother finally rising to the surface. "Really, Mother, you've already hired the top florist in London. I don't see why you insist on making the bridal bouquet, of all things."

Arabella did not look embarrassed by this outburst. "Darling, I want the world to see how much I love my only daughter."

"*Hello!* magazine, more like," Verity mumbled under her breath, but I heard her. If her mother did, she gave no sign of it.

"The roses will, of course, be of excellent quality." I paused, choosing my words carefully. "But I should probably explain that we have planned the course to demonstrate how to do two flower arrangements suitable for putting in a vase." It had never occurred to me that someone would want to make their own bridal bouquet.

Arabella chuckled pleasantly. "I'm sure it's not so different."

I knew better but since the Tudor Rose was one of my biggest customers, I decided that to keep their patrons happy, I'd find a way to turn Arabella's arrangement into something more wedding-suitable. "We'll make it work," I conceded, and tried to ignore a penetrating look from Imogen, who knew darn well she'd be the one creating the wedding bouquet. I suspected that Arabella Ainsworth might not be the easiest person to please.

"Wonderful," said Arabella, who'd clearly not considered that things wouldn't go her way. "It's going to be a simply fabulous weekend. I've been planning this mother/daughter getaway before the wedding for weeks. I thought it would be wonderful to spend time with Vee before the big day."

"Mum!" Verity exclaimed. "Please. I'm twenty-nine years old. Not five."

Again, Arabella seemed not to hear. She continued, "Hugo, her fiancé, and his best man and business partner, Jasper, are also spending the weekend. They'll be golfing at the local golf resort while we take your course. It will be a good break for all of us."

"I thought we were going to a spa," Verity said, frowning. "You said we'd get facials. And what about couples massages?" Frankly, in that moment she definitely sounded more like a petulant five-year-old than a woman of twenty-nine.

"In the afternoons, yes, darling," her mother replied. "You haven't read the schedule properly. Now, about these roses." Confidently, she walked towards Imogen and the buckets of roses she'd spent the morning carefully preparing. Leaning down, she gathered a few blooms in her hand and inspected them carefully. Honestly, you'd have thought she was a judge at the Chelsea Flower Show. "Hmm, good," she said to no one in particular. "These really are quite fresh." She peered up at Imogen. "I imagine these have been freshly-cut?"

Imogen arranged her expression in what I knew to be a specially-crafted smile for overly inquisitive customers.

"Very," she said. "We source our roses from the best growers and inspect every bloom ourselves."

Arabella looked pleased at this answer. "And have you been working with flowers for a long time? You look so young."

I had to stifle a smile. It was both a compliment alongside a subtle suggestion that Imogen was too young to be a pro.

"I have a Master Diploma in Professional Floristry," Imogen replied. "And I was an apprentice at Liberty London Flowers, where I arranged bouquets for a range of very discerning and well-known clientele." Imogen never boasted but I couldn't blame her for letting Arabella Ainsworth know she'd arranged bouquets for some pretty high-level customers.

Arabella's eyes lit up and I could tell she was dying to know what celebrities Imogen had encountered at one of London's most prestigious department stores. But despite loving gossip, Imogen herself was discreet when it came to work. She would never tell.

I glanced over at Verity, who had been busy typing feverishly on her phone. She was now staring longingly at the door, obviously desperate to leave.

Arabella continued, "I've convinced my dear friend Gillian Fairfax, I assume you know her well, to join our class this weekend."

"Yes, I saw she was a late addition to our list," Imogen replied.

"I thought it would be good for her to get out. Poor Gillian. She's been rather lost since her husband died. One can see it in her Instagram feed."

As they were leaving, I heard Verity say, "I really don't

think it was necessary to come to the florist." But Arabella shook her head. "My darling, it's attention to detail that made me such a success in life."

With that, they closed the door and disappeared down the High Street.

I turned to Imogen, feeling a little bemused. "Should I have known who that was? She held herself like a celebrity. Like she was used to having her photograph taken."

Imogen shrugged. She wasn't easily impressed. "Arabella Ainsworth is something of a London socialite. She knows Gillian through her late husband."

I nodded. The late Alistair Fairfax's family had been living in Willow Waters for generations, but like many wealthy landowners, he knew lots of titled families who lived in the city.

Imogen continued, "Arabella herself came from more humble beginnings and married up, as my mother would say. Her husband has a title but not much else going for him. He's known to be lazy and a little too fond of whiskey. Arabella, on the other hand, is hard-working and ambitious and she pretty much single-handedly turned the so-called family recipes of his titled ancestors into a line of biscuits, crackers, and gentlemen's relishes. It became huge and the line was bought out by a food conglomerate. *She's* the one who restored the family fortunes."

"Impressive," I said, meaning it. I knew what it took to build even a small business from scratch. To turn a family estate into a megabrand was, indeed, impressive.

Imogen nodded. "Arabella is charming and very good with money. She's a good person to have in our course. If she enjoys herself, she'll spread the word and tell all her rich friends. It could be great for business."

Imogen was right. The best kind of business came about through word-of-mouth recommendations. It was more important than ever to make sure the weekend went smoothly.

Imogen and I spent the rest of the afternoon making sure everything was ready. There were eight participants in the flower-arranging course and, despite my suggestion that as the better florist, Imogen should be leading the class, she had insisted that she didn't want to be the center of attention. Instead, she would circle round the group, helping anyone who was struggling. With this setup in mind, we'd chosen two arrangements that were fairly simple. I figured that if I could master them, anyone could. I knew that my forte was the relaxed, almost but not quite thrown-together look, but now I had the feeling that Arabella Ainsworth and her daughter wouldn't appreciate this style. No, they were the type of clients who'd want every single petal and leafy sprig to be perfection and woe betide the florist whose roses didn't behave. But with Imogen's flair for arrangement and my diplomacy leading the course, I figured we had it covered.

I was certain the weekend would be flawless. Well, almost certain...

Chapter Three

The mouthwatering scent of Hilary's cooking wafted over me the moment I entered my farmhouse. I slipped off my shoes and, treading over the refinished old floorboards, I reminded myself how lucky I was to have someone like Hilary to share my home with. I thought it would feel strange to have housemates at the age of thirty-five, but after Jeremy died, I'd needed help with our ambitious mortgage and Hilary seemed like the best option. It turned out that not only was she a fantastic cook, her background as a barrister and her current role as a mature Classics student had come in handy over the years; we made an ace team for pub quizzes *and* she had helped solve some of the strange crimes committed in Willow Waters of late. Char had joined us later, a young, restless woman who'd escaped life in a convent and gone on the road hoping to reach London. When she'd accidentally arrived in Willow Waters, I'd known straight away she was a fellow witch and taken her under my wing, so to speak. We'd also had to cope with Norman, a chatty parrot who'd turned out to be Char's familiar, to her utter annoyance. Now I couldn't imagine life without them.

I called out hello as I entered the kitchen. Hilary had her back to me, stirring some delicious concoction. I swear, if I didn't know better, I'd think Hilary was a witch just for her skills in the kitchen.

She turned as I entered and shot me a grin. "Coq au vin," she said, gesturing at the pot. "We're celebrating."

I raised my brows. "We are? What happened?"

"You know how Dawn and I have become good friends?"

I nodded. Hilary had befriended Dr. Dawn Fanning, a renowned archaeologist who presented the television show *Digging into History*. The team was currently filming the archaeological dig at Barnham House. I liked Dawn immensely; despite being a TV personality, years working outside with the land on digs had kept her quite literally down-to-earth. She never acted like a celebrity, she was warm and bright and brilliant—a perfect friend for Hilary.

"Well, with Dawn vouching for me," Hilary continued, "the crew on the dig have allowed me to volunteer so I can use the experience to enhance my Classics degree. I start with them over the weekend." Hilary's gray bobbed hair swung as she turned to me, and I could feel her excitement. "I'm going to learn so much. I can't wait."

I congratulated Hilary. This second part of her life was blossoming and I loved it for her. "I went past the dig myself earlier today," I said, recalling how it had compelled Alex to share his ongoing worry for my safety. "Maybe with you volunteering, you can try to dissuade them from ruining too much of that beautiful garden. It would be such a shame for the garden to fail next year once the dig is over."

Hilary nodded. "I agree. We must respect the earth herself as well as what she harbors through time."

I was about to ask more about Hilary's role when I heard a loud curse coming from the garden. I rolled my eyes. "I'm guessing Char is home already?" I asked Hilary.

She nodded. "She's been out there for a while. I assume tinkering with the truck you so kindly gave her and which she insists on calling Frodo of all things."

I laughed, and grabbing a cardigan from the back of a chair, wandered outside to the garden. I loved my garden. Asters, hydrangeas, salvias, and cosmos were all in bloom this time of year and their vivid pinks and purples of all hues and petals of all sizes brought me no end of joy. But the sense of peace my garden brought me was short-lived.

Char wasn't tinkering with the truck in the garage as I'd expected. Instead, she was squatting down beside a flower bed that was tumbling over with dahlias—a flowerbed which I knew that our magical gnome Yasmin favored. I'd bought Yasmin last month from a salesman at Woolfeder Gnomes—a family business that began in Germany, but was now expanding into the southwest of England. I'd fallen for her and ordered some gnomes to be sold in the gift section of Bewitching Blooms, alongside candles and cards and locally-made crafts. It turned out that at least some of the garden gnomes came to life, usually at night when the world was sleeping. Yasmin's resting face was one of innocence but the moment she became animated, well, the true playful nature of her spirit shone through. She'd obviously done something to aggravate Char (in truth, it didn't take much to aggravate Char) but as I went closer, I saw that Yasmin, despite being the recipient of Char's wrath, looked serenely unperturbed.

I sighed. Yasmin had invited a number of garden gnomes to live in my garden. At first, I'd felt touched that they'd chosen my humble flowerbeds for their dwelling. I loved seeing their characterful faces in the morning while I drank my coffee in the kitchen and looked out the window. But it didn't take long for their mischievous side to surface.

Char's parrot familiar, Norman liked to think of the garden as his domain, swooping from tree to tree, and taking a nap in his favorite ash tree. On the whole, Norman loved company, well, anyone who would listen to him, so I thought they'd provide a great audience. The gnomes had other ideas. For reasons of their own, perhaps boredom, they'd been arranging themselves into rude shapes only he would see from above. Norman retaliated the best way he knew how: by pooping on them.

I inched closer, reluctant to get involved. Yasmin was saying, "But you're a witch. Can't you come up with a spell to stop Norman from defecating on innocent maidens?"

"That is not the point of witchcraft," Char chided. "We need to learn to get along. We share this garden and we all have equal responsibility to keep it a beautiful place for everyone to enjoy. And that means no more rude words or shapes. No making trouble with Norman. You bring this on yourselves."

I nodded silently, thrilled with Char's thoughtful attempt at diplomacy among the magical. She had come so far from the angry young woman I had first encountered. Now she was an exemplary peacekeeping witch.

"I agree." I spoke up before Yasmin could start arguing.

Char spun round. "Oh, you're home," she said. Clearly, she was embarrassed at my witnessing of her softer side. She did like to pretend she was still a hardened motorcycle-riding tough girl, despite her elfin-like beauty.

Yasmin also looked a little chastened. "I'll speak to the other gnomes," she said finally, and bid us goodbye.

"Thank you for talking to her," I said to Char as we watched Yasmin's tiny silhouette saunter across the soil.

"Keeping that parrot in hand is a real task," Char said, shaking her head.

"I know, but it'll be better for you if there's a truce between the gnomes and Normie. It's going to be a long weekend." I reminded Char that not only was she going to be running Bewitching Blooms but it was also a full moon this weekend. "Which means there's a coven meeting tomorrow night."

Char shook her head. "I never get a minute to myself. Between work and witchcraft, there's almost no time for anything else." She paused. "Though I have been working on some new spells. Since I lose my keys all the time, I've been trying out some retrieval spells for lost things. It's not always going to plan. I've managed to summon three umbrellas and one boot that doesn't belong to me."

I laughed. "Well, if we see someone walking around Willow Waters with just one boot, we'll know where to return it."

Char chuckled, and then suddenly her whole demeanor changed. She stood a little straighter, smoothed back her space buns which protruded from behind both adorned ears, and reflexively fiddled with her silver rings. Without even turning round I knew what prompted this sudden and uncommon moment of self-consciousness for Char: Owen Jones.

Owen Jones was Gillian Fairfax's gardener, known in Willow Waters for his green fingers and rugged good looks. In the last few weeks, he and Char had discovered they had a lot in common and it was clear to everyone—except, of course, for them—that they were a perfect match. If only one of them would actually make a move.

"Oh, hey," Char said with practiced nonchalance.

Owen greeted us both and then set down a large plant pot with enticing-looking greenery flopping about. "I'm doing some tidying up in Gillian's garden," he said by way of explanation. "I divided some irises and thought you might like them."

I was always happy to receive the extra bounty from Gillian's garden. This wasn't the first time Owen had arrived with an offering for our garden. I couldn't help but think it wasn't only for the benefit of our flowerbeds.

He gave Char a shy nod of his head and asked if she'd like to help him plant the irises. Then his face creased in a frown. "What happened to all your gnomes? They're covered in bird poop."

Char wrinkled her nose. "Three guesses."

Owen laughed. "That pesky parrot of yours." He bent down and grabbed the end of the hose. "Here, let me help you give them a shower. We can plant the irises afterward."

I excused myself. If Owen and Char needed cleaning up bird poop as an excuse to spend time together, then so be it. I could think of worse dates. Maybe.

As I walked back to the kitchen, I reflected on how much my life has changed since coming to Willow Waters. Jeremy and I had arrived with such high hopes, but even though I'd lost my husband and would never have him back, I had found a family of sorts with Char and Hilary. And, while Alex wouldn't suit most people, he was definitely bringing this witch's heart back to life. And now I was getting to spend the weekend doing what I loved, in a beautiful setting, where a bride-to-be would add a sense of hopefulness and romance to the weekend workshop.

I couldn't wait to get started.

Back in the kitchen, I saw that my mother, Jessie Rae, had turned up for dinner. Again.

I loved my mom fiercely, even with all her strange foibles, but her tendency to drift in unannounced just in time for dinner could be a little annoying. Even though we were accustomed to Jessie Rae's behavior I still would have appreciated a heads up. However, knowing Hilary, there would be plenty of food, even if Owen decided to stay.

As I walked in, I heard Jessie Rae's Scottish accent roll Hilary's name around her tongue and then tell her that her instincts hadn't misled her and dinner smelled delicious.

"Hi, Mom," I said. She was wearing an orange velvet smock and several loops of pale blue glass beads wound round her neck. Her red, hennaed curls were tied back with an emerald-green chiffon headscarf. She kissed me on both cheeks and then drew back, giving me one of those looks that I had come to dread. She was here with a message from the other side. Jessie Rae's talents lay in communing with the dead—a gift that had fascinated and unsettled me in equal measure since I was a child.

I guided her away from Hilary, who was now setting an extra place at the dining table.

"What is it?" I asked her in hushed tones and steeling myself for some confused messaging. The spirits rarely speak in a straightforward manner. I was used to my mom floating around speaking of all kinds of prophecies with her gift for foresight, but some were more pressing than others. For example, it wasn't necessary to rush over here to tell me there would be frost in the morning, as she had so urgently done one time.

"Oh, my luvvie," she whispered, "the spirits have been very active today, very active."

"Did they say anything in particular, Mom? I do know they like to chat." Like some other people I could mention.

Jessie Rae began to sway a little, as is her way when communing with the spirits. Luckily, Hilary just thought my mom an eccentric and paid us no mind.

"It's unclear why they're so restless, no doubt the full moon plays her part, but Peony, you should be on your guard. I keep getting a warning about how roses are beautiful, but their thorns can tear the flesh."

My stomach dropped and a strange sensation came over me.

I looked at my mom. Not once had I told her that the flower arranging workshop this weekend was centered around roses.

I began to worry that maybe this weekend wouldn't go as smoothly as I'd hoped.

Chapter Four

Saturday morning Imogen and I headed out nice and
early to the Tudor Rose Inn, leaving Char in charge of
Bewitching Blooms for the day.

The Tudor Rose was the nicest inn for miles, featuring a
restaurant that had a Michelin star, a spa, and some of the
most gorgeous guest rooms I'd ever seen. While renovating
my own farmhouse, I'd spent hours drooling over the Tudor
Rose Inn's website, flicking through photos of the different
rooms and suites. The décor was sympathetic to its rich
history as a coaching inn since the late 1400s. Loads of
famous people had stayed there, including kings and queens
and movie stars. If only one day I could decorate the farmhouse with such gorgeous fabrics and finishings.

The Tudor Rose Inn was also a big part of our business at
Bewitching Blooms. Every week, we took four large and spectacular arrangements up to the inn. Quite often, we were also
called on to do the flowers for whatever weddings took place
at the Tudor Rose, which were numerous and lavish affairs
with adventurous centerpieces. We also delivered huge

numbers of single Tudor roses, which were red on the outside and white on the inside, with a piece of fern. In a simple vase, one of these adorned each of the dining tables.

Imogen and I parked at the delivery entrance and began to unload the van, heaving the heavy buckets of blooms one by one to the private dining room where we were to conduct our course, returning for the boxes of tools and accessories on the ground.

With everything unloaded, I took a proper look at the space. The events manager had given us the Damask Room, one of two private dining rooms at the Tudor Rose Inn. It was a charming room, stonework repointed and matched with neutral cream walls and light spilling in through mullioned windows. There were several square wooden tables that could easily seat two or three people each. One larger, rectangular table was set up at the front of the room which we could use for the demonstrations. I'd brought along some floral waterproof tablecloths to protect the tabletops from damage and I spread these across the tables. Imogen began unpacking the boxes and assigning a bundle of materials for each student.

As we were setting up, Sophia Greer, the manager of the Tudor Rose, came through the door. She was a friendly woman in her mid-forties, well-suited to hospitality, and more organized than a colonel in an army. "Morning, you two," she called out in her breezy voice. "The room is coming together nicely." She cast an eye over the roses and nodded, obviously checking out the quality of the blooms, though not in as obvious a way as Arabella Ainsworth had the day before.

"I'm very pleased with how the weekend is turning out,"

Sophia said. "Everyone taking the course is staying with us, apart from Gillian Fairfax and the two friends, Jo and Helena, who live nearby, though I believe one of them has booked a massage at the spa, and Gillian is having a facial. Plus, they're dining here. We get enough compliments from people who stay here about the flower arrangements you bring each week that I thought it might be fun to offer a flower-arranging weekend. I'm so pleased you were able to do it."

"It's my pleasure," I said. "I'm so glad you're happy."

Although we were being paid a fee, I knew it was also in the best interests of my business to keep a good relationship going with my most lucrative customer. Plus, I liked working with Sophia a lot. As the Brits say, she's a good egg.

Sophia said, "I was wondering if I could borrow you for a moment, Peony. I'd love your expert opinion on some autumn plantings we've had done on the terrace."

I looked at Imogen, not wanting to leave her in a lurch. But she gave me a smile and nod like, *I've got this, obviously,* so I told Sophia I'd be happy to.

We walked out onto the terrace, and I took a moment to appreciate what a beautiful, sunny September we were having. It was such a bright, golden morning, that I had a pang of longing to share it with Alex, quickly followed by a pang of sadness as I remembered that I wouldn't see him until next week. It was just the downside of dating a were-wolf, I guess. There had to be a few.

A handful of guests were on the terrace, enjoying their breakfasts in the fresh air. I immediately spotted Arabella Ainsworth and her daughter Verity. And then I saw she was sitting with Tamsin Mortimer, who I'd recognized while at lunch with Alex, as well as the handsome man who'd left her so abruptly, and who I'd figured for her husband. The tiff they'd been having must have been resolved, since they looked very peaceful, all sipping from tall glasses of orange juice.

Sophia was about to steer me in the direction of the new plants when Arabella spotted me and called me over. In a quiet voice, Sophia said, "Don't worry, there's plenty of time to talk plants later. Best to keep our customers happy." She slipped away, ever the amenable host.

I walked towards the table, which was positioned in a quiet corner of the terrace and shaded from the sun by a cream canopy. It had been cleared of plates, but there was a coffee pot on the table. Arabella waved at me and asked if she could pour me a coffee. As much as I loved a caffeine hit, especially so early on a Saturday morning, I didn't want to linger at the table while Imogen set up the room alone, so I declined.

Arabella shrugged and then said, "Peony, we're so excited about today. Let me introduce you to Tamsin Mortimer, Verity's best friend." She paused, and I shook Tamsin's hand. Her grip was firm, her skin smooth and dry. I had no idea whether it was appropriate to mention I'd enjoyed watching her on British Ballroom or whether I should keep my mouth shut. I decided on the latter. As she'd been voted off the show, and acquired a stalker, she probably didn't want to be reminded.

Then Arabella waved a hand in the handsome guy's direction and said, "And this is Hugo Robinson, my soon-to-be son-in-law and Verity's fiancé."

I stared at Hugo. Thank goodness I hadn't accepted the

coffee, as I'd have dropped that cup straight onto the terrace. When I'd seen Hugo and Tamsin at the country inn, my senses had screamed that those two were passionately, intimately involved. Had my witchy intuition been on holiday that day? Maybe I'd been too wrapped up in my feelings for Alex and had gotten my romantic wires crossed. Looking now at Verity, I hoped that was the case. What I'd seen at the inn was probably a perfectly innocent outing, a best friend and a fiancé planning a special surprise for Verity, perhaps, and disagreeing about the details. But still, there was a niggle of discomfort gnawing away at me.

"Are you sure you won't join us?" Arabella asked.

"I'd love to, but I've got to get back to setting up our room."

"Right, right, we mustn't be late," Arabella said with a smile. She glanced down at her phone to check the time and then I realized that every one of us was clutching a phone.

Arabella said, "It's half past nine now. Time to finish our coffee and freshen up before class."

"And we tee off at ten-thirty," said a deep male voice behind me.

I turned to see a tall man with eyes so dark they seemed to be glittering like the night. Like Hugo, he had floppy hair, but it was dark like his eyes and gleaming with some kind of gel. A sculpted beard accentuated his razor-sharp cheekbones, and he held himself in a way that announced great confidence. He was a man who was used to commanding a room. He was kitted out in pristine golfing attire in muted shades of gray and mossy green.

"This is my husband, Jasper Faringdon," Tamsin said.

"He and Hugo run a hedge fund together," Arabella

added, clearly proud of the dynamic duo. Hugo stood and then I saw he was wearing diamond-patterned golfing trousers paired with a bright blue polo shirt. He pulled on a red cap. Next to Jasper, he looked infinitely more light-hearted. "More importantly, we play a mean game of golf." He flashed a bright smile at his mother-in-law-to-be, but I suddenly sensed that golf wasn't the only mean game that Hugo liked to play. He was probably cutthroat in business meetings.

"Well, the weather is certainly fine for it," I said, glancing up at the sun and hoping that would put a swift end to the polite chitchat. There was something off about these two men and I wanted to get out of there and back to flowers.

Hugo obviously felt a pressing need to get on with his golf as well as he bent down to kiss his fiancée. "Right, good luck with the flowers, darling," he said.

"Don't you want coffee, Jasper?" Tamsin asked her husband.

He shook his head. "I'll grab something at the golf club."

"Poor Jasper," said Arabella, "It's such a shame you missed breakfast because of work. It seems criminal to work on a weekend."

"It was only a call I needed to take. I was sorry to miss you all this morning, but I'll join you for dinner."

Tamsin frowned. "Don't forget the couples massage we've got booked for 4pm," she reminded him. "I know what you're like when you get into something. You lose all track of time."

"I wouldn't miss it for the world." He gave her a kiss. All seemed harmonious between the couple but I couldn't shake my sense of unease.

Verity said, "Let's get a group photo before you go." She pointed to me. "You'll take one of all of us, won't you, Peony?"

"Of course."

But with surprising force, Tamsin yelled out, "No! I'll take the photo." She paused, her expression suddenly twisted. "Though it would be best if Jasper isn't in it, either."

Verity looked embarrassed, like she should have known better than to make the suggestion in the first place. "Oh, poor Tamsin. Are you off social media again?"

Tamsin nodded and a bitter look came into her eyes. "That crazed stalker has turned up again. I can't believe he's already out of jail. His sentence should have been much, much longer. He completely ruined my life."

My heart immediately went out to Tamsin. I had read how her stalker hounded her, finding her home address, following her to rehearsals for the British Ballroom, to restaurants and cafes, and friends' houses. Although she'd never given a public statement about her stalker, her publicist had confirmed that Tamsin had been the victim of stalking and that she asked only for privacy at this time. I also valued privacy as a basic human right and the idea of it being violated so intimately gave me the shivers.

But Jasper didn't appear to share this view. Instead, he shook his head again, clearly a little frustrated with his wife. "Darling," he said, in a tone not suited to the endearment, "you saw a dark-haired man outside the house. I'm certain you're letting your imagination run away with you."

Her voice barely audible, Tamsin murmured, "I know what I saw. It was Malcolm Pritchard. I would know that man anywhere."

Tamsin seemed nervous and suddenly self-conscious. I

felt that she was telling the truth, but no one around her was taking it very seriously. Verity looked a little bored and Arabella was already tapping away on her phone. Were they simply used to Tamsin's woes with her stalker, or could it be that she'd been using it to gain attention from her circle? Clearly, this was what Jasper seemed to believe, as he continued to encourage his wife to be included in the photo. But Tamsin was firm. She was off social media and that was that. She didn't want her photo online—anywhere.

She stood up and moved away from the table. I cleared my throat, feeling a little awkward, but took Verity's phone and snapped a few photos of Arabella, Verity, and Hugo. I handed the phone back. No doubt all the photos would turn out great; those three had won the genetics lottery.

As the two men walked away, Tamsin said bitterly, "It's all right for *him*. No one threatened *his* life."

In a soothing tone, Arabella said, "That man didn't really threaten your life, dear." The ease with which she said this made me certain this was a well-worn topic. Tamsin dramatically claiming to be afraid for her life while those closest to her remained unconvinced.

Tamsin shook her head angrily. "He sent me a message that said life was pointless if he couldn't be with me. Am I the only one who sees how threatening that is?"

In the same tone, Arabella murmured, "Of course, it's been difficult for you. I quite see that."

I noticed that Verity hadn't weighed in. In fact, she hadn't even looked up from her phone since I'd returned it. Her long pink fingernails were furiously tapping at the screen, and I suspected that she was busy editing the photo to make it even more perfect than it already was before posting it on social media.

I studied Tamsin's face. She was bitter now, great frown lines appearing in her brow and a stormy look in her eyes. She said, "I'm in talks with my agent for a very exciting opportunity, but if I can't be visible without fearing for my life, then my career is finished."

With a fleeting glance at Verity, she added sulkily, "And I don't have a trust fund to fall back on."

Grabbing her silver-cased phone from the table, Tamsin began to walk away. If Verity had missed the look, she knew that Tamsin's snide comment was directed at her. I could see she was about to snap back, but Arabella put a hand on her daughter's arm. "You know she doesn't mean to insult you, darling. She's frustrated, that's all."

Verity raised her eyebrows. "I didn't ask for a trust fund. And anyway, you're paying for her to come here. *And* all her expenses as my matron of honor. You'd think she'd be grateful."

Arabella sighed. "She is grateful, in her way, but Tamsin doesn't like to be beholden to anyone. She's very ambitious, you know, and wants to make her own way in the world. She reminds me a little of myself when I was younger."

"Yes, I know," Verity said through gritted teeth. "No doubt you wish she'd been your daughter instead of me." With that, Verity stood and flounced off towards the hotel reception.

I felt embarrassed to have witnessed so much drama. I'd been wanting to excuse myself for the last five minutes, but with all the drama among those four, I could barely get a word in.

Arabella rose gracefully to her feet. She placed a gentle

hand on my arm and said, "It's just wedding nerves. They'll both be fine by the time class begins. I am very excited to learn how to arrange flowers myself, especially with decent staff so difficult to find these days."

I nodded and forced out a smile. The day had hardly yet begun and already there was friction. Any dreams I had of a serene and beautiful weekend were dissipating as quickly as a plume of smoke from a snuffed candle.

Chapter Five

✻

Trying to shake off my mounting unease, I was heading for the back door when I noticed an unusually good-looking guy. Not that I'm interested in that kind of thing—my heart was firmly elsewhere, but he was the sort of man impossible *not* to notice. His thick black hair was cropped close to his head, and he had expressive eyebrows above wide eyes, which had a melting quality to them like hot cocoa. He looked to be in his early thirties, and his broad-shouldered frame was draped in a luxurious dark blue knit tucked into dark blue jeans. He was about to step out onto the terrace when he paused—something inside the hotel caught his attention. His gaze was transfixed until he stepped back, opened the door wider, and then Gillian Fairfax walked through. She looked her usual glamorous self, wearing a soft cream cashmere sweater paired with a cream silk skirt and brown suede kitten heels. Her blonde hair lay in gentle waves down her back, and gold earrings glittered at her lobes. Of course, I admired Gillian's style, but it was hardly an outfit appropriate for arranging flowers. She murmured thanks as she passed the handsome man, and I saw the look of interest they exchanged. He was still holding the door open long after she passed, unable to take his eyes off her.

At that moment, Gillian spotted me and immediately smiled. I waved and she approached me, kissing the air beside my cheeks. She smelled like white roses, and I briefly wondered if she had matched her perfume to the weekend's event.

"Lovely to see you, Gillian," I said, meaning it. Although Gillian and I were very different, there was a soft and thoughtful side behind the lipstick and stilettos. I'd enjoyed getting to know it over the past few months since her husband Alistair Fairfax had passed away. "It was a surprise to see your name on my list."

Gillian laughed. "Peony, I don't know what possessed me to sign up for a flower-arranging class, honestly. You do such a good job and deliver fresh arrangements to me every week. Well, I do actually. Arabella Ainsworth is very, very persuasive when she wants something. She's got it into her head that I need something to fill my time. But it's not like I sit around all day watching daytime TV."

I laughed. "I can't imagine you do," I said. Though I also couldn't quite imagine what else she did all day.

Suddenly, I realized we weren't alone. The handsome man had appeared beside Gillian. In a deep, warm voice, he asked, "Are you here for the flower-arranging class, too?"

Gillian's eyes lit up. "Too? Are you taking it as well?"

The man laughed, revealing perfect white teeth. "I am. Couldn't think of a more pleasant way to spend a weekend."

Gillian looked delighted by this answer. I could almost

read her mind: handsome *and* sensitive. Not a common combination.

He held out his hand. "Lucas Chen."

"Gillian Fairfax."

Feeling like I was intruding for the second time that morning, I introduced myself to Lucas as his teacher. He barely pulled his eyes away from Gillian to shake my hand. I glanced at my watch. "Well, you two, you've got about fifteen minutes before class if you want to grab a coffee."

"Perfect," Lucas said, breaking into an effortless smile. "Would you care to join me, Gillian?"

I was expecting the answer to be a resounding yes, so was surprised to see that Gillian looked torn. I followed her gaze and saw that Arabella was waving at Gillian to join her. "Another time," she said graciously, and you didn't need a witch's intuition to tell that she meant it. "I'll see you both inside."

It was unlike Gillian to ignore the attentions of a gorgeous man, especially a younger one. I wondered what sway Arabella had to convince her to join their table instead.

Hoping that this morning wasn't a sign of complicated dynamics to come, I took a deep breath of the gorgeous autumnal air and began to make my way back to the Damask Room. I didn't get very far. The moment I stepped into the corridor, Sophia appeared. She looked pleased as she said, "Ah. Peony, we've just had a late addition to the class. Or at least a request for one. It's Frederick, Roberto's husband, who owns the coffee shop. Do you know him?"

I nodded. I'd met Frederick perhaps a handful of times. He was a successful painter and often away from Willow Waters at artists' residencies across Europe or showing his work at fancy galleries in London. With his artistic flair, I was sure he'd be wonderful at flower arranging, maybe even an inspiration to the others, and it would be nice to get to know him better. I told Sophia as much.

She beamed. A late addition was good for her business too. "So, we can squeeze him in?"

I nodded. "With pleasure. I brought extra equipment and flowers in case of any accidents."

"Smart thinking," she said, and gave my arm a little squeeze. "I'll check in on you later."

By the time I made it back to the Damask Room, two women had already arrived. They were wearing almost identical twinset cardigans and slacks and had positioned themselves at the table nearest the front.

"Good morning," one said brightly, self-consciously touching her shiny brown bob. "I know we're early, but I've been an early bird since I was a girl. I always loved school. I liked to get there early and get a good seat at the front. Teacher's pet, my father used to call me, only joking, you know." She let out a titter of nervous laughter. From her eager, anxious expression, I could already tell that she'd want a lot of reassurance and encouragement.

She continued, "I'm Josephine Bennett, but everyone calls me Jo. I can see you're Peony Bellefleur from your photo on the flyer for the course. And this is my friend and neighbor Helena Gill."

Helena whispered a hello, clearly the shy one in this little duo. She had auburn hair, a fraction shorter than her friend, and wore large tortoiseshell glasses.

"Good morning," I said, "Lovely to meet you both." I glanced at Imogen, but my efficient florist had everything arranged and was already making sure all the tables had plenty of supplies.

One of the hotel servers entered with jugs of water and glasses and set them down on the front table. I thanked her and then checked my watch again. It was ten minutes to ten. I figured the rest of the group were still drinking coffee and trying not to squabble with one another. Helena stood and came to the front and in a meek voice asked if it was okay to pour some water. "Of course," I said, a little taken aback. "Please, you must make yourselves at home. We're here to relax and have some fun as well as learn a new skill."

Helena nodded shyly and poured a glass for herself and one for Jo. As they settled into their chairs, I was somewhat alarmed to see them take out notebooks and pens, fussing over them as if they were going to write an entire book about floral arrangement. Maybe this weekend was going to be more serious than I'd intended.

I asked both ladies why they'd decided to take the course. Jo answered first. "I'm a keen gardener, you see, and I want to have the skill to arrange my own homegrown flowers."

"Oh, how lovely," I said. "There's nothing like a bouquet from flowers you've grown yourself. I love to pick flowers from my own garden and arrange them for the kitchen and hallway." This was good. My easy breezy way with flowers would suit Helena very well.

With a blush, Helena told me that her daughter was getting married in the spring. "It'll be a small, intimate wedding," she explained, a little breathless with excitement, "So I wanted to help out by doing all the flowers for the church. If I'm brave enough, I might even do her bouquet."

"What a coincidence!" I replied. "There's a bride and her

mother taking the course who wanted some tips on bridal bouquets. Now I can give you both some handy hints."

Helena looked thrilled and I was pleased, as well as a little relieved, that I'd be able to cater to Arabella's goal for the weekend without alienating the rest of the group.

Next to arrive was Frederick, Roberto's husband. Frederick was the kind of artist to truly live his work and his appearance reflected this. He had a penchant for monochrome, oversized garments and today he was wearing black smocked trousers with a white linen shirt which billowed magnificently as he moved. He had an incredible eye for detail, and I noticed immediately that his chunky silver cufflinks matched the hoop which hung in one ear— a contrast to his closely-shaved head. Not to sound too much like my mom, Jessie Rae, but he had an aura of creativity and openness, which manifested in his demeanor and body language—he was fluid as he moved about the room.

"Peony," he said, reaching out to grasp my hands in his, "thank you so much for taking me on as a late addition to class." He kissed both my cheeks. "I've been in Venice and only just found out about this weekend with flowers and said to myself, how could I not take the chance to immerse myself in roses?" His blue eyes twinkled. Then he lowered his voice. "But please, dear Peony, don't tell Roberto. I want to surprise him with a fresh arrangement that I've made myself for our anniversary on Monday." He gave me a conspiratorial wink. "He thinks I'm at my studio."

I assured Frederick that he could count on my discretion. He flashed a charming smile at the two ladies and settled himself at a table to the side and back.

Jo immediately swivelled in her chair and asked Frederick if he was a gardener.

He let out a soft laugh and then held up his hands, which I saw now were covered in gray paint. "An artist," he said, "mainly with oil paints but sometimes I work with multimedia platforms. I love flowers and often use them in my work."

I looked over at Frederick, surprised. I realized now that I'd never actually seen any of his work before. "You do?" I asked.

He nodded. "Oh yes. My latest series, *A Rose is a Rose is a Rose* uses the flower as a starting point but then transforms them into abstract shapes, colors, and patterns that I hope evoke the essence or emotion of the flower as opposed to its realistic appearance. I think maybe I'm entering my Georgia O'Keeffe era. I just love the way her paintings of flowers are rendered in sweeping curves and dramatic compositions. Such energy."

"Oh, how wonderful," Helena said quietly. "You sound just like a real artist." Frederick gave her a funny look. He *was* a real artist. But I could see he wasn't really offended.

Next to arrive were a married couple who introduced themselves as Kent and Grace Hildebrand. They looked to be in their sixties, although a sense of vitality and strength emanated from their tanned and weathered faces. They both wore head-to-toe athletic gear. Grace's brown hair was pulled back into a neat ponytail and something about her purposeful stride as she headed for the back table made me think she was a seasoned runner. Kent was maybe a few years older. His broad shoulders and defined arms were probably the result of a serious commitment to weight training. His dark hair, flecked with hints of gray at the temples, gave a distinguished quality to his otherwise youthful appearance. I figured he was the kind of person who could be found cycling up challenging hills on weekends or doing a set of pull-ups with effortless precision. As a couple, they had great synergy.

Next came Arabella with Verity, and a few steps behind them was Tamsin, who was just ending a phone call. Her phone's silver case caught the light and glimmered for a moment. Tamsin looked less than thrilled; I had trouble discerning whether it was because she didn't really want to be here (just like her best friend, Verity) or if her phone call had been unpleasant.

"Good morning," Arabella trilled out, addressing the whole room. She frowned a little, seeing that so many of the class had already made themselves at home. I figured she was used to arranging things as she liked them.

"Please take a seat anywhere," I said, gesturing toward the tables which were still free.

Arabella chose the table in the middle of the room. As Tamsin took a seat beside her, Jo suddenly said, "You look familiar, dear. Do I know you from somewhere?"

My heart plummeted for Tamsin, since it was pretty clear from what I'd overheard earlier that she wanted to be anonymous, but before Tamsin could even reply, Frederick said, "Why, it's Tamsin Mortimer. I followed your tennis career and was there when you won at Wimbledon. What a game. You were absolutely magnificent, my dear."

I watched Tamsin's face as a light entered her eyes. To my relief, she was obviously cheered up knowing that she had a devoted tennis fan in the room. A whimsical smile played around her lips. "Wimbledon, 2018. I remember the heat and how difficult that last game was. But it was one of the greatest days of my life," she admitted.

"You do look familiar," Jo said and then turned to Helena. "But I don't watch the tennis. Do you?"

Frederick smiled. "Even without tennis knowledge, you'll likely recognize Ms. Mortimer from British Ballroom last year." He turned back to Tamsin. "Your *paso doble* was breathtaking. The sensuality, the athleticism." He sighed. "I was captivated."

"Oh, that's it," Jo squealed. "I saw you on the telly. I don't know how you do it, week after week, learning new dances and then performing on television. And those judges, they must frighten the life out of you."

Half-whispering to her friend, Helena said, "I can't believe I didn't see it straight away. *Of course* it's Tamsin Mortimer. Wasn't she the one who had the trouble with the police?"

Much louder, Jo repeated, "Trouble with the police?" She looked over at Tamsin, alarmed.

"I'm sure I read that in the papers," Helena said.

"I had an overenthusiastic fan," Tamsin said shortly. "A stalker, to be more precise. He went to prison for six months." She paused. "But not before I was forced to leave British Ballroom."

"But weren't you voted off?" asked Helena. "I was certain you were."

I swallowed. Hopefully Helena had more talent at flower arranging than she had tact.

Tamsin looked furious but I could see she was trying to keep her emotions in hand. In an even tone she finally said, "You try competitive dancing on television while a madman is stalking you. You'd find your focus was impaired too."

Chapter Six

Helena, realizing her faux pas with Tamsin, looked like she wanted the ground to swallow her up. She turned a violent shade of beetroot and mumbled an apology under her breath. Luckily, the door opened at that moment and Lucas Chen swaggered into the room. The tension dissolved as everyone took in the handsome man who simply flashed his white teeth and gave the room a nod as if to say, *Yes, I am here now. All is well.*

Really, it was quite astounding what an attractive man could do to a room.

"Have a seat anywhere you like, Lucas," I said.

I watched as he surveyed his choices. He clearly noticed the empty seat beside Frederick but chose to sit on his own at the only remaining empty table. His eyes trained on the door and I knew he was waiting for Gillian, who walked in at one minute past ten. He flashed her that winning smile and gestured towards the chair opposite his. Gillian gave the room a small smile, murmuring good morning. Then, instead of joining Lucas, she walked over to Frederick, who stood and air-kissed her hello and then fetched her a glass of water. I was surprised that Gillian hadn't chosen the seat beside Lucas, but I imagined she had her reasons.

With Gillian completing our little group, it was time to begin. Taking my position at the front of the room, I introduced myself and Imogen and went over the schedule briefly: Class would run from ten a.m. to twelve p.m., then we'd break for lunch, and class would resume again from one p.m. to three p.m. When we'd finished for the day, everyone was free to enjoy the hotel even if they hadn't booked a room for the weekend. As Sophia had asked me to, I mentioned that there were still some spa treatments available for the afternoon and they could book them during the lunch break if they hadn't already.

"As we're going to be spending a nice chunk of time together," I said, "I thought it would be nice to get to know each other before I start teaching. I'll go first. As some of you know, I was born and raised in the USA. I arrived in Willow Waters a few years ago and soon after opened Bewitching Blooms and began selling flowers and gift items. I've loved every moment of living and working in the village and feel passionate about the power of flowers to transform a home, lift a mood, and show friendship or gratitude to others." I paused, realizing I sounded quite earnest. But it was all true. I did love my job and I did believe in the power of flowers.

I gestured at Imogen, who stood up from behind the table and came to join my side. "This is my trusted colleague, Imogen Poots. She's a remarkable florist and I'm lucky to have her."

Imogen, who was usually so composed, flushed a happy shade of pink. She quickly recovered her poise, however, and launched into her prepared speech. "I grew up in Willow Waters, leaving the village briefly to study and train in London. I love to incorporate locally-grown flowers with the exotic blooms we also bring in. Every day at Bewitching Blooms is different. I never know who is going to walk through the door or what kind of creation they'll be after. It keeps my job fresh and exciting."

It was lovely to hear Imogen talk this way, and I thanked her and then said, "Who'd like to go next?" I would have put money on it being Arabella, but Lucas Chen spoke first.

"Hi, everyone," he said. "My name is Lucas, and I grew up in Hong Kong and England. I still love to travel as much as work allows me. By day, I'm an accountant but in my spare time I grow roses as a hobby." I'd been in England long enough to discern different accents and I could tell that he'd had an expensive education. He gave Gillian a pointed look, which she chose to ignore. Inwardly, I grinned. After her disastrous love life lately, either Gillian had vowed to stay away from men for a while or she was an expert at playing hard to get. For now, I couldn't tell. But despite my dislike of village gossip, I *was* intrigued to see where this would go...

Kent Hildebrand went next. He explained that he was retired now but used to run a kayaking business with his wife, Grace, who left her homeland of the Netherlands to join him in the Cotswolds. Smiling, he said, "When I'm not kayaking, I'm the kind of person who can be found cycling up mountains on weekends or wild swimming. I don't like to sit still."

His wife laughed. "That's very true. As much as I also love the great outdoors, this weekend is my attempt at getting Kent to slow the pace a little. I want us to find a balance between challenging ourselves physically and enjoying life's simple pleasures. We're thinking of purchasing a florist shop as a retirement project. We'll employ staff, but I want to learn a bit about flower arranging so I know how best to run the business. Plus, it's a cliché I know, but I grew up surrounded by the most perfect tulips and I want to learn how to work with flowers to brighten our home."

"That's wonderful," I said, happy to have a tulip enthusiast in the mix. "I'm sure we can give you some special tips for tulips, as well as roses."

"I'm quite partial to a tulip myself," Jo said. "The parrot ones are my favorite. I just love the way they look like they were cut with pinking shears. So pretty. Anyway, I'm Jo, and I work in HR at a fishing company based in Dorset. Been there for twenty years. My real passion is gardening, though, and I just love to learn. I'm always taking courses. I've done a bit of pottery, some crochet, even a week of life drawing." She glanced at Frederick. "I never knew how difficult it was to be an artist." He bowed his head to her. "As you might be able to tell, I am a bit of a chatterbox but I take my classes seriously. I'm happy to be here and I'm sure we'll all be the best of friends by the end of the weekend." She paused for breath and smiled brightly at everyone. I discerned an eye roll from Gillian, but everyone else smiled back politely.

There was a brief silence and then Jo jabbed Helena in the ribs.

Quietly Helena said, "I'm not sure what to say. I'm Helena. I'm Jo's neighbor. I work in the office of a primary school and I love my job. I treated myself to this course because my daughter is getting married next year and I want to arrange the flowers for the church myself."

At that Arabella called out, "But that's wonderful. We're both mothers of brides hoping to make lovely bouquets for our daughters to carry." She beamed at the room. "This is my daughter, Verity, the beautiful bride."

Verity looked mortified. "Yes," she said, "that's me. The bride." Then she drawled, "Among many other things my mother has forgotten."

"Oh, but darling, you know how proud I am of you," Arabella said quickly. "It's just I've dreamed of your wedding day since you were a little girl."

"Isn't it supposed to be the other way around?" Verity said, sulking.

At that Arabella laughed and then gestured at Tamsin. "Well, we all know who Tamsin is. She also happens to be my daughter's best friend. And I'm Arabella. I wanted a bonding weekend with the girls and, like Helena, I'll also be doing the flowers for my daughter's wedding."

Verity said, "One bouquet, Mother. You're making one bouquet." She looked around the room. "In addition to the very important task of being a bride, I work in a London gallery called Lucent Studios. We showcase up-and-coming British artists." She stopped and glanced at Frederick.

He chuckled. "No, no, my dear. I'm not represented by your gallery. I'm afraid I'm not up-and-coming. More like been-and-gone."

Some polite laughter rang out.

Tamsin's phone beeped loudly and she finally looked away from its screen to apologize. "It seems you all know who I am," she said. "To be frank, I've come along to get away from my home where I definitely saw my stalker. I'd very much appreciate it if all of you can keep me out of any photos or posts. My being here is entirely secret. I'm sure you understand."

"Of course," Jo said. "I'm so sorry for your troubles. But if he's been to prison, let's hope he's learned his lesson."

A dark expression clouded Tamsin's face. "I have a feeling that there are some people in this life who never learn their lesson."

The room was swirling with emotions—some of which were decidedly negative. I didn't want to start the weekend on the wrong foot, so, while Imogen delivered a few words on health and safety and explained the fire-escape routes, I stood back and performed a silent ceremony against negative energy. It was a practice that my mom, Jessie Rae, had taught me when I was a teenage witch and in need of battling some hormonal demons. Especially at high school. I didn't miss those days.

The silent ceremony was contemplative and intimate and usually performed in a dimly lit setting as a way to create a space of peace, protection, and renewal. I didn't have this kind of setup, but I didn't let it stop me. It was the energy that was important. I needed to shift the atmosphere, dispelling all the negativity and instead creating a more harmonious environment.

I entered the meditation by envisioning a rose rising up in front of me. I chose a white rose, bright with luminosity. Its plentiful thorns were sharp and pronounced. When I could see it clearly, I placed all my attention on its form. This was to be my psychic protection—for myself and my cohorts—and I envisioned my own body behind that rose, zipping myself up psychically to protect myself from negative energy.

I silently repeated a personal mantra, *In this moment, I am calm. I am present. I am at peace.*

And then I turned my attention back to the room, focusing on the energy that all of these people were generating together.

When I finished, the atmosphere felt noticeably lighter and there was a palpable sense of renewal. Most of the negative energy had been dispelled but I also sensed a powerful resistance. I followed its energy to Tamsin and then sighed. She was back on her phone and frowning. Although the man who had been stalking her was nowhere in sight, he was dwelling in her mind and weighing heavily on her soul. It would take more than a silent ceremony to rid Tamsin of his spirit. I would have to find a way to get closer to her and help her on this journey. Maybe I could imbue one of her roses for the arrangement with a sense of calm and renewal.

Chapter Seven

I mogen finished her health and safety speech and now it was my time to step into the limelight.

I took a deep breath and called to mind all that I had prepared the last few weeks to guide my new students in my chosen craft.

"Flower arranging is both an art and a science," I began, "blending creativity with an understanding of floral design principles. Imogen and I are going to talk through the basics of these principles over the next two days and these will help you to create two beautiful arrangements here at the Tudor Rose which you'll be taking home. But by the time the course is finished, you'll be able to draw on this knowledge every time you make a bouquet from flowers picked from your gardens or purchased."

I paused to smile at everyone.

"The first, and probably hardest, thing you have to do is choose your types of flowers. You'll want to select a mix of focal flowers, filler flowers, and greenery. By focal flowers, I mean the statement blooms of your arrangement. Today we'll be using roses, but depending on the season you could choose lilies or orchids. Anything that has panache. Then you'll want to choose some fillers, like Gypsophila paniculate, more commonly known as baby's breath or Limonium sinuatum, also known as statice, to plump out the arrangement, or you can stick with greenery to add texture and volume. It will all depend on your personal style."

Jo and Helena were making notes, their hands flying across the page with impressive speed.

"Of course, this will all depend on your color scheme, which you'll want to plan in advance. You might want to consider complementary or analogous color schemes. For two of you here, soft pastels are mostly used for weddings, as they tend to feel the most harmonious, but don't think you can't stamp your own personality on your arrangement."

Frederick raised his hand. "I definitely want a bold color scheme." He laughed and turned to Arabella and then to Helena. "I can be the male yang to your female yins."

I joined in with the laughter. "You'll be surprised how different your bouquets will look at the end—even working with the same flowers." I gestured at Imogen. "We work with the same blooms every day at the shop but create completely different arrangements. Our styles are naturally different. I couldn't copy Imogen's artistry, that's for sure. If she put her mind to it, I'm sure she could imitate my style. But what I'm trying to say is that floristry really is an art form. One that anyone can enjoy."

"But it's also practical," Imogen said, suddenly coming to life behind the table. She glanced at me, waiting for the nod to continue. I was overjoyed that she was feeling confident enough to contribute to the talk.

She cleared her throat. "Once you've chosen your flowers, how you prepare them is just as important." She stood and gathered a bunch of gorgeous blooms which we'd chosen for our demonstration. "First, you cut the stems at an angle to create a larger surface area for water absorption." She picked up the flowers and demonstrated how best to trim the stems. "How much you take off will depend on your arrangement's size and your desired overall length."

I nodded again, encouraging her to continue. Now that she was handling the flowers, Imogen seemed to have all but forgotten she had an audience. I couldn't stop the smile on my face as I watched her. Imogen was a natural teacher. Next, she showed the group how to properly strip any leaves that would be submerged in water to prevent decay. "Leaves in the water can introduce bacteria, shortening the life of the arrangement," she explained.

Grace Hildebrand's hand went up. "I was hoping to know more about how to lengthen the lifespan of fresh flowers. That's a useful tip. Is there anything else you can suggest?"

"That's a great question," I said. "I'm glad you asked." I explained that a lot of people often set their vase of arranged flowers on a windowsill or mantelpiece in direct sunlight. "Of course, it's a very pretty position for flowers, especially if the window is looking out onto a garden. It gives a room that inside-outside feeling. But, actually, you should always keep the flowers in a cool place, away from direct sunlight or heat sources. If you change the water every two or three days and re-cut the stems, you'll prolong the life of the arrangement."

I continued, "Since we're focusing on roses, you should know that a professional florist will do something called conditioning, soaking them in water for several hours before arranging to ensure they stay hydrated."

I looked around the room. All eyes were trained on me. Except for Tamsin's. She was still preoccupied with her phone, barely listening. It was likely she didn't want to be here at all and had just been dragged along by Verity and Arabella. No. That wasn't it. Just Arabella. Verity was watching but her eyes were unfocused. She was bored. I tried not to frown and not worry about them too soon. Surely as the morning went on, Verity and maybe even Tamsin would have their imaginations captured.

Imogen began to demonstrate how to handle the prepared flowers. We'd agreed to begin with a more simple, undone arrangement which I'd demonstrate today. Now that she was feeling more confident, I would hand over the more complicated arrangement to her tomorrow.

Imogen passed me the cut stems and I said, "My style is all about creating a natural flow by arranging the flowers in a way that guides the eye through the design. This can be achieved by varying stem lengths and spacing." I began by placing the largest and focal flowers first. "These should be at the center or slightly off-center to draw attention," I explained. "Then we use smaller flowers or greenery to fill in gaps and create depth. These shouldn't overshadow the focal flowers but complement them. You can create a layered look by placing flowers at different heights and angles, giving depth to the arrangement."

I explained that it's a good idea to take a step back every so often to view your arrangement from different angles. "We can make adjustments as needed to balance the design, adding or removing flowers as we go."

Finally finished, I stepped back for the final time. I said, "With practice, you'll develop your own style and techniques for flower arranging, but following these basic principles will give you a strong foundation."

Arabella's hand went up. "What factors do you consider when creating a bridal bouquet beyond it complementing the bride's dress and wedding theme?"

"Oh, that's a wonderful question," Helena said. To Jo she whispered, "I wish I'd asked that."

It *was* a good question. One which showed an understanding that a bridal bouquet was more than just a collection of flowers—it was an expression of the bride's individuality and the overall wedding vision. "You want to think of ways to create something which reflects her personality and style. For example, I can see by Verity's nails that she prefers a matte finish to a glossy one. You could include more flowers with a soft, nonglossy finish to their petals, as opposed to a shiny or waxy texture. Matte flowers have a more natural, understated look, often giving them a more organic, earthy, or vintage feel. You could include certain varieties of roses, peonies, ranunculi, and dahlias."

Arabella beamed. "Oh, what a wonderful suggestion. Thank you. I just adore ranunculi."

I wondered what flowers her daughter adored, but it didn't seem like Arabella was too concerned with her daughter's taste.

It was time for my students to start their work. "Feel free to follow my demonstration," I said, "but change the arrangement according to your own personalities and desired outcomes. Imogen and I will come round and help as you go."

As the group got to work, I felt relieved. I'd managed to remember most of what I'd planned. What's more, as I walked around the room, I realized I was actually having fun. The tables were transforming into canvases of vibrant colors, and the blooms' gentle fragrances, along with the tang of greenery, filled the air. Most of the group worked with quiet focus, snipping stems and shaping their designs. Sunlight streamed in through the casement windows, casting soft, golden light across the space.

Only Tamsin was struggling. She'd finally put down her phone but her flowers kept wilting. She made a sound of frustration, and Arabella asked, "Do you have particularly hot hands?"

"No," Tamsin said, sounding insulted. But I suspected the wilt in her roses had less to do with her hands and more that her psychic energy was so negative that the flowers were wilting in response. I went over to offer some encouragement and breathed a quick spell to perk up her flowers.

Jo couldn't stay quiet for long, however, and soon called Imogen over to ask for guidance. I noticed Helena looking over at me for approval as she nervously arranged a small, simpler bouquet. I went to her side. "It's really starting to take shape," I said, guiding her hand as she placed a rose.

Helena blushed. "I'm just practicing this morning. Hopefully by tomorrow, I'll be able to make something more special for my daughter."

I smiled. "I'm sure you will."

Lucas was a little clumsy but he was earnest in his approach. I let Imogen help him, as she clearly didn't mind getting a little closer to the handsome man.

A faint hum of conversation started as the group began to

admire each other's work and offer encouragement. There was a peaceful rhythm to the work: cutting, arranging, adjusting, and stepping back to assess.

As I expected, Frederick was a natural. He stood next to Gillian, utterly absorbed in his work. He'd chosen brighter colors than the others, vivid magenta and the deepest red roses, expertly combining the flowers into what I could tell would be a dramatic centerpiece. Gillian was also focused, though she obviously worked on the principle that more is better. I watched as she stabbed large quantities of roses into her foam without once asking for guidance.

Arabella had her head down, working with intensity on her bouquet. Now I could see that she was in earnest about playing this part in her daughter's wedding. And while there might be ego behind the decision, she was working hard to learn the technique. The bouquet would be one mother's handmade gift to her daughter. I was touched. Watching her fingers manipulate the blooms, I went to the bucket of white roses and quickly breathed a spell of romantic love on the stems Arabella would later add to her bridal bouquet.

I noticed with interest that the Hildebrands were making sure not to waste anything. Maybe all their time outdoors had made them more conscious about sustainability. They worked carefully and slowly, building the smallest arrangements of the class.

Noon came around quickly. I could see that most of the group, except for Tamsin, of course, were tired from standing on their feet so long. I told everyone to finish where they were for now and said we'd take an hour's break. "We'll reconvene at one p.m.," I said, "and I'll talk more about how to know when you're finished and how to add finishing touches."

"Ah yes, a little lunch would be perfect about now," Frederick said, and handed Gillian her handbag. "Would you do me the honor of joining me?" he asked.

"Of course, darling," she said, linking her arm through his.

Poor Lucas looked entirely crestfallen.

As everyone gathered their things the door opened and Hugo and Jasper appeared. Their golf outfits looked very out of place in the Damask Room, and they also looked as fresh as they had at breakfast.

Beaming, Hugo said, "We've come to take you ladies to lunch."

Verity looked confused. "But you're supposed to be playing golf," she said.

"Had to postpone," he replied, shaking his head. "Business. We moved our tee-off time to half past one so we can join you for lunch."

Then Hugo looked worried. "Wait, it's not bad luck for me to see the wedding flowers before the big day, is it?"

Jasper laughed and patted him on the back. "If it is, then you're in grave trouble, my friend."

Chapter Eight

A fter the group left (Jo and Helena ironically the last to leave although the first to arrive) I poured two glasses of water and collapsed onto a damask chair alongside Imogen. Until I finally sat down, I hadn't realized how much teaching had taken out of me. Speaking at length, paying unerring attention to each member of the group, whispering quiet spells left, right, and center—not to mention trying to ward off Tamsin's negative energy. I was spent.

Still, I thought it was going well and said as much to Imogen.

She nodded. "I think so, too." Then she paused. "Though there are some weird vibes, too. I mean, Tamsin doesn't seem to want to be here at all. I also can't understand why Lucas is here either, though I'm not complaining. He's easy on the eye."

I laughed. Imogen was usually quite coy about her dating life, but you didn't have to be a witch to know when she thought a man was interesting. I sat back in my chair and did a few arm stretches, trying to relieve some of the tension that had built up from bending over so many tables.

Imogen took a long drink of water and then said, "I don't believe for one second that Verity will let her mother anywhere near her wedding flowers. Do you?"

I shrugged. "Maybe not. Perhaps they're really here for the spa, the massages, and Michelin-starred restaurant."

"And Tamsin has been dragged along for the ride?"

"I think Tamsin agreed to come so she could stay out of sight because of her stalker. She probably didn't want to be at home in London." I left out the bit about seeing her cozy at lunch with Hugo. I still hadn't quite figured out what had been going on there.

Imogen lowered her voice. "I had to really play it cool when I saw Tamsin Mortimer walk in. I'm a huge fan of British Ballroom. I just adore the costumes and the choreography. All that glamor and beautiful routines. Plus, the competition is really compelling. You can never tell from how the celebrities dance at the beginning who might evolve and become a star."

I admitted I hadn't watched all of it. I tended to sit with Hilary when she watched the show so I never really got into the competition. "I remember Tamsin dancing the jive, I think it was. Very fast and athletic."

Imogen raised one of her perfectly shaped eyebrows.

"I can't believe you didn't watch all of it. Tamsin's series was incredible. The competition was fierce but because of the tennis, I suppose, Tamsin had this totally natural aptitude for movement and rhythm. She wasn't the best dancer at the start, but she had good posture and footwork, and she was so dedicated that every week she made visible improvements no matter what dances they threw at her. Ballroom, Latin, she mastered it. You could see the raw ambition which had made her a tennis pro."

"Sounds like she was set to win."

"She was definitely a favorite. But then it all went wrong."

"The stalker."

Imogen nodded gravely. "Part of Tamsin's appeal was that she knew how to capture the audience's attention, not just with her dancing, but with her personality. She was charming. Demure despite her ambition. I reckon that's exactly what attracted her stalker. She's very charismatic, don't you think? When she's not on her phone, that is."

"Do you know much about him? The stalker, I mean. I read a bit, but she seems really spooked."

Imogen admitted she'd kept up with the story in the papers. "It started off pretty harmless, sending her fan letters and flowers. The kind of thing you'd expect to happen to a celebrity on the show. But then he started hanging around outside the rehearsal hall, waiting for her to come out. He'd try to give her gifts in person, but Tamsin has said publicly she never accepted them. Then it escalated. He began to message her online and then he found out her address. He sent letters at first, which grew increasingly passionate. But then he started loitering outside her house. She called the police, but they couldn't do anything because he always stood on the opposite side of the street. In her statement, she said she felt like a prisoner in her own home. His behavior persisted. He began to follow her more places. She saw him in the supermarket, at restaurants. She stopped going out at night. Finally, he crossed the line and knocked on her door. Tried to force his way in. He was arrested and sent to jail. But the sentence wasn't very long at all. I think it was six months. And now it sounds like he's been released. Do you really think she saw him hanging around outside her home?"

"I think she believes she did, though her husband and friends seem skeptical." I shook my head. "It sounds awful." Poor Tamsin. I did feel for her. Not just because I'm a witch dating a werewolf so the idea of being followed was a nightmare, but also because I believe that everyone should have the right to lead a private life without judgment from others. How awful to have a total stranger latch onto Tamsin and follow her places.

It was annoying that Tamsin was on her phone the whole time, but I understood completely if she was worried for her safety. I wondered again why Arabella and Verity weren't taking her fears more seriously.

Imogen stood and we began to tidy up the morning's mess, making sure each table was reset for the afternoon. There was a gnawing in my stomach. Unlike Arabella's group, there was no Michelin-starred lunch coming my way. I was about to stop work and pull out the sandwiches I'd made for us when the door opened and Sophia arrived, carrying a silver platter with a domed lid.

She beamed at us and then lifted the lid. "I thought you two might be getting hungry, so I had the kitchen rustle up a little something." She set down a platter filled with an assortment of sandwiches, a pot of steaming tea, and a plate of what looked to be freshly-baked shortbread.

"Please, sit and eat," she suggested, and then began to stroll around the room, admiring the half-finished arrangements, each with their own design. "I can't believe these were all done by novices. You're excellent teachers. I did overhear the group chattering in the dining room. They're positively buzzing about the workshop."

"How lovely," I said, thrilled that things were going so well. "Are they all sitting at the same table?" I wanted to know if my little spell had brought the group together and they'd be a more harmonious bunch after lunch.

But Sophia shook her head. "The bridal party and the two men are eating together; the Hildebrands and Jo and Helena have chummed up on another table. And Gillian and Frederick are about as far away from the rest of the group as they could get. But then Lucas came into the dining room and Frederick gestured for him to join them. Lucas seemed very pleased."

I nodded. Of course, Lucas was pleased. He'd given his arrangement a good go, but his wandering eye hadn't gone unnoticed. I was surprised the poor guy didn't have whiplash from all the rubbernecking towards Gillian's table.

Sophia excused herself and said she must get back to work. Imogen and I hungrily tucked into lunch. The generous spread didn't last long. We'd both worked up a real appetite. Imogen said she'd pour the tea and I went out to the bathroom to freshen up before the afternoon session began.

The Tudor Rose was full of long, winding corridors, tastefully decorated with gilded wallpaper. As I made my way to one of the restrooms, I inhaled the faint scent of wood and polished leather. The restroom was right at the end, but I stopped in my tracks as I heard two women frantically whispering inside.

One voice was slightly louder. I recognized it immediately despite the anger which distorted its tone.

It was Arabella.

I took a step closer as she said, "I can't believe it. How could you betray us all like this?"

I had a sinking feeling that I knew exactly who she was talking to.

Chapter Nine

A s I hovered, just out of sight of the restroom, my stomach turned and I braced myself, not wanting to interrupt the conversation but finding it impossible to walk away.

And then there was Tamsin's voice, high with outrage. "I don't know what you're talking about."

Arabella drew a deep breath and snapped, "You were *seen*, Tamsin. You've become sloppy."

"Please," Tamsin said, "enlighten me. I haven't the foggiest what you're on about." Her tone was thick with sarcasm and I couldn't help but feel she was on the defensive.

"I've just been informed by someone *very* reliable that you and Hugo were seen together at a place called The Orange Tree."

There was silence. I held my breath, wondering what Tamsin would say next.

Eventually there was a light and awkward smattering of laughter. "Oh, Arabella, that was nothing. Hugo and I are planning a special wedding surprise for Verity. We were meeting there to talk in secret. There's nothing untoward about it. We didn't tell you what we were doing as you're not exactly the best at keeping things quiet."

More silence.

I waited. Would Arabella accept this excuse or would she be even more offended? Maybe Tamsin was telling the truth. I know I'd felt a romantic connection between her and Hugo but sometimes, just sometimes, I could be wrong about these things.

"No," Arabella said. "Your 'meeting,' as you call it, was not to plan a surprise for my daughter." Real venom came into her voice as she spat, "You were seen kissing Hugo. Now try to tell me again the two of you have my daughter's best interests at heart."

So I *had* been right. The intensity between those two was sensual. I hadn't seen them actually touching each other, but they may as well have been with the sexual tension that oozed from them both. Not to mention the heated way Hugo had stormed out. It had definitely looked like a lovers' tiff.

But Tamsin was not about to be backed into a corner. With a surprising neutrality to her tone, she replied that whoever this person was, they were mistaken.

She was about to say more but Arabella cut her off. "No, Tamsin. No more lies."

There was a long pause and I got the sense that Arabella was trying to steel herself for what was coming next. When she spoke, it was with a steady voice. "I've known about you and Hugo for some time now. The two of you are not as clever as you think."

I imagined the look of surprise on Tamsin's face and wondered if she felt at all guilty about her affair with her best friend's fiancé. Not to mention the betrayal of her own husband.

Arabella, getting into her stride now, said, "I can see the way Hugo looks at you. I know when a man desires a woman." She continued, "It sickened me, of course. But I assumed the shine of something new would wear off and you'd both see what a terrible mistake you were making." There was a pause. "But it turns out that you're both more stupid than I thought. I'm not going to keep turning a blind eye to this nonsense."

Even through the door, I could feel Tamsin's indignation rising. It was hot and sharp and full of fury. I couldn't tell if she truly loved Hugo and wanted to defend their affair, or if she was simply offended.

After a moment, in a quieter voice, though no less full of malice, Tamsin said, "Why would you want Hugo to marry Verity when he loves me?"

"Don't be a fool. Hugo is perfect for Vee. He comes from the right family and he is amassing the kind of fortune that will keep Verity in the lifestyle she's accustomed to. And you have Jasper. Or are you forgetting that you're already married? End this now. Or I will. One way or another."

I swallowed. The confrontation was not just about the affair anymore— It was about power and control. And who had it. Arabella didn't appear to be seeking revenge or even just seeking answers. She had already reconciled herself to the truth. It was up to Tamsin to make the next move. The ball was, for now, in Tamsin's court. Would she smash it as far as she could with her famous backhand so that it would disappear from the court altogether? Or would she bide her time, keeping the ball close to her chest?

I sensed that this was the end of the conversation and quickly slipped away from the restroom door before either woman realized that they'd been overheard. I stepped into an empty conference room and listened for the sound of the two women's footsteps to disappear before I came out again.

I breathed hard, unable to help feeling perturbed. So much for my harmonious spell to bind the group. So much for breathing romance into Arabella's blooms. Instead, the romantic connections had completely lost their way. And what about Verity? I hadn't exactly warmed to the bride-to-be, but I wouldn't wish her position on my worst enemy. There was no worse betrayal than your best friend and fiancé having an affair. And now the truth was even more painful than I'd imagined with her own mother knowing the truth and not telling her. I couldn't help but wonder if Verity would want to marry Hugo if she knew. Why was her mother letting this wedding go ahead? How could she want Hugo as a son-in-law, knowing that he was cheating on her daughter? Surely his position and family money couldn't be that important.

I shook my head, though there was no one to answer my questions. It was hard to believe that warm and friendly Arabella was so calculating beneath that bright exterior. Though perhaps that's why she was so successful at business. She'd had to be driven and determined to transform her husband's fortunes. Perhaps the same drive had leaked into her private life, permeating what should be protected with love.

With the coast clear, I finally went into the bathroom to freshen up. I splashed some cold water on my face and spent a moment staring back at my reflection. I looked worried. The tensions of the group had gotten under my skin, and I couldn't shake the feeling that something awful was about to happen. If that was a confrontation between the two best friends, it would be a horrible showdown of betrayal, loss and wounded egos.

I slipped a brush from my bag, undid my practical pony-tail, and ran the brush through my hair. I'd let my brown hair grow long over summer and now it lay in a sheet beyond my shoulders. I gathered the strands again, pulled them back into the hairband and refreshed my lip gloss. I had a course to run and this was a time for business—not getting caught up in other peoples' drama.

By the time I returned to the Damask Room, the students had already started to drift in and resettle in their places. I noticed Lucas was sitting on the edge of Frederick and Gillian's table, rather than his own. Gillian was laughing at something Lucas had just said. Her pale blue eyes were sparkling, full of genuine warmth. It looked like their lunch had laid the foundation for a real connection. I only hoped that if it did turn romantic, as Lucas obviously hoped, then Gillian would have better luck than normal. Her love life for as long as I'd known her had been a car crash, and although Gillian hadn't always made the wisest choices, I wished her the best. But then Gillian caught me watching them and suddenly stiffened up. To Lucas she said, "Perhaps it's time you went back to your table. It looks like we're about to begin."

Lucas was immediately crestfallen, looking around the room and seeing it was still only half full. We were still waiting for the Hildebrands and the bridal party—and to be honest, I wasn't entirely sure Tamsin would reappear.

But to my surprise, the three women returned as one

group. Tamsin looked sullen, a little paler than earlier, but otherwise there was no indication of the showdown I knew had just taken place.

Arabella was the epitome of collected cool. Her pink lipstick had been refreshed, and she was glowing and smiling. She really was a master of projecting an image.

And Verity? She looked exactly the same. No hint of trouble marred her expression. She stifled a yawn and I thought her uppermost emotion was boredom.

When everyone was settled, I welcomed the group back and said I hoped they'd all had a lovely lunch.

Frederick called out, "Most delicious." And there were murmurs of agreement from the rest of the group. Only Tamsin remained silent. I was going to have to work hard not to let the negative energy spiraling from her body infect the others. As soon as I had a moment, I would recite another spell. A stronger one this time. Though my magic, potent as it was, would find it difficult to penetrate such a torrid love triangle as this.

I arranged my face into a bright smile and then explained that the afternoon would be all about finishing touches. I suggested that they make use of the small sprigs of lavender and the purple and white wildflowers to encourage a sense of undone elegance to the final bouquets. Imogen and I would circle the group and show them how to finesse their work. Without any further fanfare, I told the group to return to their arrangements.

I'd planned to discuss with Imogen how to split the room for help, but since I took longer freshening up, I gestured for her to choose where she'd like to go. It was no surprise she went to Lucas first. But Imogen was a consummate professional. There wasn't a suggestion of flirtation in her interaction. As I went to help Helena, who was feeling unsure about her greenery, I could hear Imogen telling Lucas he needed to stand farther away from the arrangement to properly assess its composition, making sure that every flower had its place, and that the color, texture, and shape were all properly balanced. I watched as she gently reached for a stray stem, adjusting it to make a slight bend. "The style Peony demonstrated should feel natural, like it could have been plucked from a garden just moments ago." She stood for a moment in silence, contemplating the bouquet. Then she took three delicate sprigs of greenery and showed him how to tuck them into the gaps to give the arrangement depth.

Lucas stood back and appraised his creation. "It's still missing something," he said.

"You're right," Imogen agreed.

And then, glancing over at Gillian for a moment, he took another white rose—a gorgeous specimen—and made it the standout piece. It was perfect. And it was how he saw Gillian. I smiled to myself.

But Imogen had caught the look. I saw it registering across her face. If Lucas was into older women, then Imogen wasn't about to compete in a losing battle.

I turned my attention back to Helena. Her hands were a little unsteady, still lacking confidence. I guided her to make sure the flowers' heads were facing outward, open to catch the light. Her friend Jo was also after some pointers to finesse her colorful arrangement. It was a little haphazard, so I suggested trimming the stems to make sure they were the perfect length for its vase.

We continued this way for some time, circling the group,

offering suggestions and answering questions. It would have been a perfect afternoon, if not for Tamsin's glowering. She had lost interest in her bouquet entirely. But Imogen, unaware of what had happened at lunch, was patiently trying to explain how best to finish. Arabella continued in the same jolly mood with which she began the day and, to her credit, even Verity focused and was on her way to finishing a quite decent-looking bouquet—even if it was a little rose-heavy.

It was Gillian, however, who surprised me the most. Her arrangement showcased the deep red roses I was so proud of sourcing. She had made the most of the rich, velvety shades of crimson by placing them in a loose, organic formation, with all the flowers slightly tilted in different directions, nestled among cleverly-placed greenery, as though they'd just been picked from a sun-dappled garden. Only Gillian and Frederick had used the trailing eucalyptus to add a touch of silvery blue, and she had made the most of its lacy edges to create texture in her bouquet. It was romantic and lush and full of whimsy.

When Frederick excused himself to use the restroom, I went to her and quietly (so as not to offend the rest of the group) told her how impressed I was with her bouquet.

She glowed in response and then said, "To be honest, I've surprised myself! I thought this course would just be a nice way to spend a weekend. But I've been so absorbed in what I've been doing I haven't noticed the time pass at all. It's simply flown by."

I smiled. I couldn't have hoped for a better reaction to the day. I felt eyes on us and turned to see Lucas staring at Gillian again. In a soft voice, I half-whispered, "You really do have an admirer there."

Gillian gave a coy smile but gently shook her head. Whispering back, she said, "I'm staying away from young, good-looking men. I've had enough drama with them to last a lifetime."

I understood what she was saying but there was something different about Lucas, a sincerity that was palpable.

Maybe there could be a happy ending to Gillian's love life after all.

Chapter Ten

It was time to end class.

I was thrilled with how the first day had gone and impressed with the vast array of bouquets everyone had created. Pretty much the whole group had made something very beautiful, though Kent Hildebrand had taken the 'undone' part of the bouquet a little too literally. I instructed everyone to tidy up their workstations and Imogen walked round with a bag for loose ends of ribbon and stray cuttings.

As the group packed up, I told them that tomorrow we'd work on a more formal arrangement with the option to have extra guidance for bridal bouquets.

Helena clapped her hands. "Wonderful," she said, and Arabella cried out, "I can't wait."

I was happy that the two mothers of brides were thrilled. But I couldn't help but notice that Verity was less so. I was determined to get her to enjoy herself this weekend. With all that was happening right under her nose, I felt a deep sympathy for her, even if she was a little sullen.

Tamsin's phone trilled; after glancing at the caller ID she

waved a hand at me, which I assumed was her way of thanking Imogen and me for the day, and then hurried out to take the call.

Everyone else was still packing up, and we'd brought boxes for them to put their arrangements into. Tamsin's flowers sat on the table where she'd left them.

Arabella frowned at Tamsin's bouquet, which she'd barely bothered to finish. I felt bad that she'd paid for her daughter's bestie to take this course when Tamsin obviously wasn't getting much out of it, but I felt even worse that she knew Tamsin was betraying Verity with her fiancé and had no intention of stopping the wedding, or at least informing her daughter of the affair.

As Imogen walked round, she appraised the final results. I could tell that she was genuinely pleased with everyone's progress and was also feeling a little bit proud of her own teaching skills. She said, "You've all made lovely bouquets. For those of you staying here, you can take them up to your rooms in their vases. And for the locals, you're welcome to take them home and we'll store the vases here. With our tips to help extend the life of your bouquet, they should give pleasure for the week to come and then some."

There was a round of thanks from the group and then they filtered out, smiling and clutching their bouquets proudly.

When the room was empty, I gave Imogen a high-five.

"A resounding success," I said. "Thank you for being such a brilliant teacher. You're a natural."

Imogen sighed, looking relieved. "I enjoyed it so much more than I thought I would. And everyone worked hard. Well, almost everyone." She glanced at Tamsin's bouquet, which had been left behind. It was somehow sadder than the rest and, despite my spell, the flowers were already beginning to droop again. A full moon should have made my spells more potent. Instead, they were struggling to overcome the tensions which were rampant in this strange set of friends. I couldn't figure out why. Surely I wasn't losing my touch? Or was there something darker at work here that I didn't know about?

Then I saw that Tamsin had also left her handbag on the floor by her chair.

I picked it up, surprised by how heavy the small brown leather bag was. I told Imogen I'd find Tamsin and hand over the bag and then come back to help tidy up.

I headed out and walked along the quiet corridors, wondering where I'd go if I wanted to take a private call. I went towards the delivery entrance and found Tamsin, who was just ending her call.

I waved and when she saw me, she looked relieved.

"Oh, thank you so much," she said, gesturing at the bag. "I'd just realized I'd dashed out without my things and was worried you might have left already."

I told her it was no problem, that we had plenty more cleaning-up to do.

Tamsin gave me a small smile. "I think I owe you an apology. I've been very distracted all day."

She paused, and I wondered with alarm if she was about to confide in me about the problem of her love triangle.

Eventually she said, "I'm in the middle of talks to be a TV commentator for women's tennis."

"Wow!" I replied, impressed. "That sounds like a great opportunity."

"It is. I mean, it's going to entail a lot of travel, but if it comes together then this will be the start of a whole new chapter in my life." She paused again. "And I think it's time for a new start."

I nodded. Whatever was going on with Tamsin in her private and public life, a new start was probably a good idea. For everyone involved.

"Thank you again for this," Tamsin said, patting the bag. "The last thing in the world I'd want is for someone to get their hands on my ID and cards." She stopped and shuddered a little, no doubt thinking about her stalker and what could happen if he was to come across that kind of information. Visibly pulling herself together, she added, "And thank you again for today." She let out a sigh. "I've got to go get ready for this couples massage now."

She sounded less than enthused. Just then, I spied Imogen, who was carrying Tamsin's bouquet in its vase.

Imogen said, "I thought it would be nice for you to put in your room." She briefly explained what Tamsin had missed from the end of class and the ex-tennis pro thanked her. Then, taking the vase, hurried off to her room.

Imogen and I walked back to the Damask Room to begin the daunting task of clearing the room and resetting it for tomorrow's class. As we tackled the remaining mess, Imogen suddenly put a hand to her chest. "Oh, I should have told Tamsin that someone was looking for her just now."

A bolt of alarm shot through me. "Who was it?" I asked, trying to keep my tone neutral. Maybe Tamsin's paranoia about her stalker was getting to me, but I hoped it had been a woman looking for Tamsin.

Imogen shrugged casually. "A man. Pleasant looking."

"Was it her husband?"

"I don't know. I didn't really look at her husband. But I got the sense that he knew her well, so it probably was. I said she'd gone to her room, so he'll have caught up to her."

Imogen went to collect the water glasses and return them to the kitchen. I began to sweep the floor, but my mind was uneasy. At breakfast this morning, Tamsin had mentioned catching a glimpse of her stalker in London now that he was out of jail. What if somehow he had got wind of her retreat in the Cotswolds? I stopped sweeping, caught between two conflicting emotions. Not telling Tamsin she'd had a man drop by looking for her could be a terrible oversight if it was her stalker. But if it was her husband, then I'd just be bothering an already-tormented person with an unnecessary interruption during her couples massage. But I immediately knew the right thing to do. The hotel wouldn't hand out guests' room numbers, but I did have her cell number on the sign-up sheet.

I found the paperwork and told Imogen I'd give Tamsin a quick call.

She picked up after one ring, a note of irritation in her voice as she said, "Yes? Who is this?"

I swallowed. So I *was* bothering her. "Tamsin, hi, it's Peony Bellefleur. I'm calling because you had someone stop by looking for you and my colleague forgot to pass on the message. I felt you should know."

Tamsin said, in a clipped tone, rigid with annoyance. "Thank you," she said. "It was my husband. He was looking for me because he had to leave the Cotswolds early. In fact, he's already gone." She explained that he only got a couple of holes of golf in before he received an important work call.

Some of his clients were insisting that they meet in London and there was no time to waste.

"Oh, what a shame he had to leave early," I commiserated.

"Business is always more important than I am," she said sharply.

I was at a loss at how to comfort her. Especially since I knew she was cheating on said husband with his business and golfing partner. "Will you still be able to have your massage?" I figured Tamsin could do with more than a little tension relief.

"Jasper said I should just tell them to massage me for twice as long since we've already paid for two."

It occurred to me that perhaps Verity had also been left stranded. I asked Tamsin if Hugo also had to leave and received a bitter laugh in return. "Oh no. He's managed to stay here and continue with his game. Between you and me, Hugo might have the money and the connections, but it's Jasper who has the brains and does all the work."

I was shocked by Tamsin's confession. And more than a little confused. It sounded like she had no respect for Hugo and yet I knew they were romantically involved. At the same time she obviously had respect for Jasper's business acumen while resenting the impact it had on their marriage. It was a sticky web those four were mired in. I envied none of them.

After ending my call with Tamsin, I went back to my broom. Imogen joined me. "So it was her husband?" she asked.

I nodded. "He's had to leave the weekend early. She isn't best pleased."

Imogen raised an eyebrow but said nothing. She was obviously keen to finish work. Together we went through the motions of tidying the room and readying ourselves for the next morning. Imogen carefully gathered up the remaining flowers and foliage, separating some that were too wilted or accidentally broken; she'd put those into compost. I wiped down the scissors, wire cutters, and the floral foam and finally cleaned the tablecloths. Imogen was itching to leave— Saturday evening was approaching, after all, so I told her I'd finish up and she could get going.

She thanked me with a quick hug and skipped off to whatever fun thing twenty-somethings did on a weekend night. But I also had important plans of my own. It was a full moon which now meant two things. I couldn't see Alex for two days, but there was the coven meeting, which went some way toward making up for it. There was nothing nicer than coming together with my sisters, catching up on the month's events, and performing our full-moon rituals. This time, it was my turn to host, as Hilary was staying with Dawn tonight after they worked late on the archaeological dig. Knowing I already had a big weekend planned with the course, I'd prepared everything the night before and Jessie Rae had agreed to cook a big pot of her famous minestrone soup and bring it over to the farmhouse.

I left the Damask Room for the day but before I'd walked more than a few steps, I spotted Verity and Hugo in matching white terry-towel hotel robes, holding hands. They made a very good-looking couple and looked comfortable and at ease with one another. My heart immediately went out to Verity, who had no idea what was happening behind closed doors.

Verity gave a friendly wave. "Finally time for some pampering," she said.

"Couples massage?" I asked.

Verity nodded. "I could really do with it after standing on my feet for so long."

I knew what she meant. I was aching all over. But pampering for me would be a hot bath filled with herbal salts, not an expensive massage at a fancy hotel. I glanced at Hugo, who smiled warmly. He looked just as happy and contented as his fiancée. He seemed equally as emotionally connected to Verity as he had to Tamsin. It occurred to me that he might be one of those men who can compartmentalize women. Not my favorite kind of man.

However, if Verity discovered the intrigue going on behind her back, she risked losing both her fiancé and her best friend.

Chapter Eleven

B ack at the farmhouse, I had that hot bath but didn't soak as long as I'd have liked. I had a coven meeting to prepare for. I rushed round, plumping up cushions, turning on all the cozy lamps, and making some final touches to the many vases of flowers I'd dotted about the place. I'd fallen in love with the old farmhouse at first sight. It was a true place of charm and mystery, with ivy climbing up its old stone walls and herbs spilling out of every corner. Although I didn't do it often, I loved hosting the coven meetings and filling the large house with the sound of laughter and urgent chatter. It felt like that's what the old building wanted.

Tonight, the energy in the air felt electric—a fitting backdrop for a night to honor the Harvest Moon and celebrate the season's bounty. Char had been practicing lighting the candles for the magic circle. I was so proud of the witch she was becoming and knew that if she stayed focused her powers would develop to exciting heights.

When Char arrived home, a bit later than I'd expected, I

could hardly wait to ask how her first day looking after Bewitching Blooms had been.

"Sorry I'm a bit late, Peony," she said, pulling off her Doc Martens as she came in the door.

She grinned, sensing that I was desperate to know that all had gone smoothly, and then reassured me with two thumbs up. "Today was great," she said. "The pre-made bouquets sold themselves and it was busy, but nowhere near as hectic as the coffee shop gets when it's busy. I enjoyed myself. And even Norman behaved." At the mention of his name, Normie flew into the kitchen and added, "I was an angel."

"And modest, too," I said, laughing.

I was about to ask more when Jessie Rae appeared, carrying a big casserole dish.

"Oh lordie, Peony," she said, setting the huge thing down on the stove. "I should have asked you to pick me up. I had quite the time getting here with this thing."

I looked at her in alarm. "How *did* you get here?" In the business of the weekend, I had completely overlooked my mom's inability to drive and hadn't considered how she'd manage. "I had a friend drop me," she said, rather mysteriously. "But he's a terrible driver and I almost spilled the whole thing over poor Loki." She gestured at her familiar, a small and mischievous ferret, whose little eyes glinted as he peeked out from his snug position tucked in my mom's shoulder bag. "Loki's itching to run around," she murmured, letting him down. The ferret scampered over to Blue, who opened one eye and regarded him with mild disinterest before deciding he wasn't worth moving for.

Jessie Rae huffed dramatically as she rearranged her curls and slipped off her bag. She was a vision in a deep purple tunic, silver jewelry glinting. Tonight, she looked unusually focused, her usual breezy demeanor sharpened by the energy of the full moon.

"Is everything ready?" she asked.

I nodded. We'd spend most of the evening outside in my garden to be directly beneath the energy of the full moon. "The circle is ready," I said. "As soon as everyone arrives, Char will light the candles."

Jessie Rae gave Char a warm, knowing look. Char was the youngest witch among us, still uncertain of her powers, and so tonight would be both an honor and a test.

Outside, the moon was high and full, casting a silvery glow over my garden. I'd set up a circle of chairs and cushions in the middle of the lawn and a smaller inner circle of candles, ready to be lit. The air was scented with rosemary, sage, roses, and a hint of late-blooming lavender. Blue, my lazy, marmalade-furred cat, wandered around, sniffing here and there. She seemed to enjoy watching the action of a coven circle and made for a perfect, cozy companion in magic. Norman positioned himself on a nearby garden bench, his beady eyes fixed on us with his usual look of sarcastic disdain. He wasn't one for creating an atmosphere. He was more of a doer. Which of course was why he got himself into trouble all the time.

I felt a familiar hum of anticipation as we waited for the rest of the coven to gather. We didn't meet as often as we'd like, what with everyone busy with their own lives, shops, and secrets. But the full moon always pulled us together, a reminder of our shared purpose and bond.

Amanda arrived first, carrying a wicker basket filled with homemade breads, cheeses, and jars of chutney from her deli. She was a sturdy, down-to-earth woman in her early forties, with dark hair cut into a practical short style and a warmth to her smile that always made me feel instantly at ease. Amanda's magic was as comforting as her food, solid and grounding—a necessary counterbalance to some of our wilder energies.

"Brought a little feast for us," she said, as she placed the basket on the kitchen table. "Figured we could use it after the ritual."

"You're a treasure, Amanda," I replied. Everyone usually brought something to eat or drink, but I knew Amanda's bread alone could make any gathering a success.

Next came Lucille, our resident potion-maker and preschool teacher. She had a whimsical look about her—messy strands of silver-gray hair, half-hidden beneath a large floppy hat decorated with dried flowers. Lucille was in her fifties but seemed to be aging backward, her energy effervescent and her laughter infectious. She had a knack for whipping up potions that could heal, soothe, or even bring a sense of joy when needed. Tonight, she'd brought a bundle of herbs from her garden, tied with a ribbon. The scent of rosemary, thyme, and mint wafted from her as she greeted us with a bright smile, along with her elderflower cordial.

"Got us some herbs to throw on the fire later," she said, waving them around. "For gratitude and blessings."

A few more witches completed the circle—two more local friends who added their own flavors to our motley coven. There was Edie, a practical woman with short-cropped silver hair who had a way of cutting through nonsense like a knife through butter. Edie owned a small farm nearby and specialized in earth magic—she could grow anything, anywhere, and often used her abilities to help local farmers with their crops. And finally, Bronwyn, a soft-spoken healer who ran a small herbal shop on the edge of town. Bronwyn was tall and willowy, with an ethereal quality about her, her long dark hair braided with tiny flowers. She moved like a breeze, quiet and graceful, and her presence always brought a calming energy to our gatherings.

With everyone settled in, I lit a bundle of sage and walked the circle, wafting the smoke around each member, cleansing our space and welcoming their spirits. As the smoke drifted skyward, we began our ritual for the Harvest Moon.

Char stood and, without a hint of the nervousness I knew she must be feeling, closed her eyes and used her magic to light each waiting candle, murmuring the words of the spell beneath her breath. She performed perfectly. When she opened her eyes, she smiled at her success and then took a seat. I was proud of my protegé.

Amanda spoke first, leading us in a grounding exercise, her voice calm and steady as she guided us to connect with the earth beneath us. Each of us placed our hands on the ground, feeling the coolness of the soil, letting the energy of the land fill us.

She said, "We gather here under the light of the full moon to acknowledge the lunar shift and set our intentions for the month coming. This night is particularly special because it's a Harvest Moon—its rise happening at nearly the same time for several nights in a row. For generations, our sisters have viewed this moon as a symbol of abundance, prosperity, and the end of the growing season. The Harvest Moon, with its large, bright appearance and its association with the changing of seasons, reminds us to stay connected to nature,

NANCY WARREN

to observe the cyclical passage of time, and remember we are in a time of transition. It marks the approach of winter, a time when the earth begins to slow down and rest. Its rise signals the end of the intense growth period of the year, leading into a season of reflection and preparation for the colder months ahead."

Next, Lucille stood and tossed a handful of her herbs into the fire, murmuring words of gratitude for the season's bounty. The flames crackled, flaring a bright green for a moment, filling the air with the sharp scent of rosemary and thyme.

Char spoke next, her voice softer, unsure, but earnest. She expressed her hopes for guidance in finding her magical path, and we all murmured our encouragement, supporting her on her journey.

Finally, it was my turn. I stood in the center of the circle, holding a bundle of late-blooming roses and lavender from my shop. I murmured a blessing for abundance and protection, then tossed the flowers into the fire. The flames leapt high, bathing us all in warm light, and I felt the energy of the moon above us—bright, watching, protective.

My mom stood. She held up her hands, her eyes half-closed as she began to chant, her Scottish accent deep and mellow as she called to the spirits that lingered close on this night of the full moon. I felt a shiver run down my spine as the air grew colder, and I could sense a faint, otherworldly presence in our circle. Jessie Rae always had a way of opening the veil between worlds, and tonight was no different. But it didn't always yield positive connections. Right now I had a sense that something was about to change.

And then my mom's calm, controlled voice suddenly

began to crack. Her fingers flittered with agitation—a sure sign that the spirits were restless and had things to communicate. The energy shifted. Jessie Rae's breath became shallow and her body began to sway. She made no attempt to steady herself. Instead, I could see that she was opening up her body to receive whatever message the spirits were so desperate to deliver. The circle pulsed with an electric tension, the very air was charged with the spirits' presence.

She suddenly flinched and her eyes flew open. They were filled with confusion and fear. "No...this isn't right..." she whispered. Her brow furrowed as she struggled to understand the spirits' messages. "Please," she said, speaking with urgency, "I need to understand. Could you be more clear?" She continued to tremble.

I looked around the circle. The other witches were watching her intently. The tension was palpable. It was clear that the spirits were not at peace and my mom wasn't receiving a clear message.

She closed her eyes again and her body continued to sway. Suddenly she shouted, "Oh, oh, no. Can it be stopped?" She shuddered.

I drew a deep breath. My mom was receiving a warning.

"What can we do? It must be stopped at all costs." She frowned, waiting and listening. But whatever the spirits were saying gave her no solace. There would be no clear answers.

Her eyes opened and Jessie Rae finally returned to this world and to the circle of her sisters. She looked at us one by one, still absorbing the shock of her séance.

"Evil walks tonight, my sisters. Lock your doors and keep your loved ones close. The rose is beautiful, but beware its thorns."

A shiver went down my spine. My whole weekend had been designed to celebrate the rose. This was the second time Mom had received a message about the rose hiding its thorns. Was it a coincidence? Or was my mom's message linked to me in some way? I stared into the fire as it crackled as if I would find some answers among the dancing flames. My mother's messages from the other world were powerful, but they were cryptic. I knew she didn't have any more information. I would have to keep my wits about me.

Lucille stood then and closed the circle with a few words of hope. "My sisters," she began, her silver-gray hair free of its hat now and glinting in the moonlight, "we should end this evening's ceremony with a message of thanks and hope." She raised her arms high to the sky. "In gratitude to the elements —Earth, Air, Fire, and Water—thank you for your strength and wisdom. Return to your domains." Then, turning her hands up towards the sky, she thanked the moon for illuminating the path, for its cycles of growth and release, and for the wisdom it had shared.

I closed my eyes, feeling the pull of the moon's energy, drawing it in to give me strength for the month to come.

Lucille said, "I now close this circle, sealing the magic and the intent that we have woven together. The work is complete. The spell is cast. May it unfold with grace."

The wind stirred slightly, as if responding to her commands.

Char stood and extinguished the candles one by one, closing the energetic portals they had opened.

I breathed out as I felt our combined magic gently dissipate into the night air and the energy return to its natural rhythm.

As the fire crackled and a shiver went down my spine, Norman decided it was finally an appropriate time to chime in. "Lovely ritual, ladies," he squawked, sounding more sarcastic than sincere. "I'm sure the spirits are *riveted*."

We all laughed, the tension easing.

"Let's head inside and eat," I suggested. I tried to keep my tone light and look forward to the rest of the evening ahead, catching up and gossiping with my fellow witches. But I couldn't help but wonder what sinister message my mom had received from the spirits.

And why was it connected to the rose, that most romantic of flowers, and my chosen bloom for the weekend?

Chapter Twelve

W e enjoyed a late supper, sharing stories of magic and of our everyday lives. That final, frightening warning to Jessie Rae floated among us, never referred to but never completely absent. I tried to join in with my sisters but my mind was racing. Roses and thorns. Beauty and pain. Love and betrayal.

The image that kept coming to me was of Tamsin and Hugo at lunch, their close affection and then the way he'd abruptly stormed out.

Had they had a fight? Or had Hugo belatedly done the right thing and ended his relationship with his wife's best friend?

I so hoped he had done the right thing.

I lifted my mom's huge casserole dish into the kitchen sink and rinsed away the last remnants of her glorious minestrone soup. It was close to midnight, and one by one, my coven sisters had left the farmhouse amid a flurry of hugs and blessings.

I passed the now-clean dish to Char, who dried it, and

then I told my mom I'd drive her home, conscious of my early start tomorrow morning.

"I could do with a drive," Char said. "I can take you home."

"Are you still buzzing with energy?" I asked, knowing how excited she was to have lit and extinguished the candles, and to have been so welcomed by the coven.

She nodded. "My whole body feels like I've plugged it into an electric socket. I'm buzzing."

I laughed but I understood what she meant and could sense the energy coursing through her. I wanted to drive Mom home, mostly because I'd get the chance to pass Fitzlupin Castle, where Alex was locked away. I hoped he'd be able to sense me nearby.

In the end, Char drove and I went along for the ride. My mom lived in a tiny but charming one-bed cottage on the other side of the village.

As we stepped out into the night, I didn't know if the cold air was giving me the chills or if I was reacting to Mom's ominous message from the spirits. Buckling up, I asked Jessie Rae if she had any more details from the spirits that she could share.

I watched her in the rear-view mirror as she shook her head sadly and her red curls tumbled about her shoulders. "Och, lassie, I wish I could tell you more but the spirits. They were so frantic, so urgent to speak, that their words tumbled out in strange orders. They spoke over one another, some whispering, some shouting. It was hard to make head or tails of it. But what overrode it all was a powerful evil at loose this weekend and an urgent message to keep your loved ones close."

She leaned forward and placed a hand on my shoulder. "I'm glad to be with you tonight," she said quietly and then sat back in her seat.

"Nothing more about the roses?" I asked, trying to keep the fear from entering my voice.

Again, she shook her head. "Just to beware that behind their beauty a thorn lies, ready to prick. It was symbolic, I think."

I swallowed. I didn't want to worry my mom with a link between my weekend workshop and her message. It was possible the whole thing was a coincidence. But there was one thing that I'd learned in my time living in Willow Waters: never underestimate the potential dangers that lie beneath a calm surface.

Char was an expert driver and she easily navigated the narrow, cobbled road that wound through the village, hugging the edges of old stone cottages, their golden facades softened by the pale light. There was something so special about Willow Waters at night when the sidewalks were empty and each building seemed to whisper of centuries past. The moon cast long, silvery shadows across the lanes, illuminating the curves of the village green, where ancient oak trees stood like silent sentinels. Their twisted branches stretched up towards the sky as if reaching for the full moon. Most of the windows in the cottages were dark, but every now and then, I would catch the gleam of a television or a reading lamp. We passed The Mermaid pub, closed and dark now, its sign swaying in the breeze.

Before long, we were at my mom's cottage. Char pulled over and as I said good night to my mom, she pressed her soft powdery cheeks to mine and squeezed me hard. "Stay safe, my Peony," she whispered. "Blessed be." I swallowed. My mom almost never called me by my name. It was always 'luvvie' or 'duckie' or 'lassie.' She wanted me to take her warning seriously.

I carried in the big soup pot and made sure Mom locked the door behind me when I left. When Jessie Rae was safely back inside her cottage, I turned to Char and asked her to drive the long way home. Char glanced at me, but knew better than to ask questions. She simply nodded and put her foot on the gas.

I wound down the window a little and let the crisp night air rush in. It carried the faint scent of damp earth and ivy, which always clung to the stone walls of the houses. I usually felt a sense of absolute peace after a full-moon ritual, but tonight my nerves were jangled. I knew what I needed to see to set my heart at rest.

After a few minutes there it was: Fitzlupin Castle, Alex's family home. It had been in the Stanford family for hundreds of years and in the silver light of the moon, it was a thing of great beauty. Set back from the country lanes by way of a long private drive, the estate comprised a house, tower, and extensive outbuildings, including stables. All surrounded by a dry medieval moat. I knew that Alex had banished himself to the dungeon but I wanted to be near him, to feel his energy and the comfort that it gave me, even when we were not in the same room.

Yet as we drew closer, a chill came over me as I felt certain I could hear the howling of a wolf in anguish. I glanced at Char to see if she could hear it too. If she did, Char said nothing, her eyes fixed on the road. Her gaze was distant in a way that I knew meant her thoughts were dashing around in different directions and she was trying to bring herself back into focus.

Again, I recalled what my mother had said about keeping our loved ones close. The distance between Alex and me on these full-moon nights felt greater with each month. I missed him, even though it had only been a day, and was beginning to realize just how much comfort his presence gave me.

Again, a howl echoed across the wind but this time its tone was different. I suddenly knew that Alex had sensed I was nearby and was now feeling his confinement more acutely. I closed my eyes, took some deep breaths and tried to calm myself so I could send him calming energy. After a few moments, I could feel my heartbeat slow and I brought to mind the white rose I had plucked from the restaurant garden on Friday and imbued with calming magic. I sent him that vision using the charge of the full moon to make my magic stronger.

As we passed the castle, I was certain Alex had received my magic and the howling was less anguished. I breathed out, the relief in my body palpable. We might not be in the same room, but the connection between Alex and me could transcend walls.

I wound up the window and sat back in my seat, determined to let my worries slide and look ahead to the final day of the flower-arranging course.

Char, who'd been silent for some time, suddenly said, "Everyone around here must be rich."

I turned and looked at her in surprise. The hour was late and traffic had been sparse.

"What makes you say that?" I asked.

"Since we left your mom's, we've passed a brand new

Range Rover, a new silver Jaguar, and that's a BMW-X5 coming toward us."

I watched as the BMW passed us in a flash of blue so shiny that the car must be new. Although Willow Waters was pretty affluent, it was unusual to see so many expensive cars. "Probably tourists," I said, though it was true that lots of wealthy Londoners and people even farther afield were buying second and third homes in the Cotswolds.

We passed the Tudor Rose where I'd soon be back at work, when all at once a cloud shifted in front of the moon, so the old inn took on a dark and forbidding silhouette. I shivered and then Char asked, "Did you just feel like an ice cube slithered down your spine?"

I turned to look at her in surprise once more. "Yes," I admitted. "Did you feel that too?"

Char nodded grimly. "I think maybe your mum got under my skin tonight."

I forced out a small laugh. "She tends to do that."

Char looked out at the inn again and remarked that no doubt a place as old as that was full of ghosts. "The full moon probably makes them restless," she said, and then dropped the matter.

I wished I shared Char's ability to reach for the most logical conclusions and set my mind at rest so easily. But the fact was I had been in tune with my powers as a witch far longer than she and so placed more trust in the strange and inexplicable jolts of intuition which arose from time to time. I swiveled in my seat as we passed the Tudor Rose Inn and I saw a lit bedroom window turn dark as the place settled down for the night. I murmured a few words to bring peace to the inn but feared we were already too far away for the spell to work.

By the time we returned to the farmhouse, I was exhausted. It had been an extremely long day full of unexpected tensions. I was desperate to fall into bed but as we pulled into my driveway I spotted Norman and Yasmin by the potted hydrangeas.

Char groaned. "Don't tell me those two are fighting again."

"You have to get Norman under control," I said.

Char said, "It's all right for you. Your familiar is a sleepy marmalade cat who basically spends all day purring and snacking. Having Normie around is like trying to contain a hormonal teenager."

Now it was my turn to laugh. "Our familiars find us. They're a match for a reason. Maybe Normie was sent to develop your peacemaking skills."

Char rolled her eyes and then opened the door. "Norman," she called out, and he turned to face her with as guilty an expression as a parrot could muster.

Yasmin puffed out her cheeks and stomped her foot. "Oh, for the love of mushrooms, stop it already! I don't care what color your feathers are, and I certainly don't care about your *so-called* cleverness. You're just an overgrown crow with a mouth like a windmill on a stormy day!"

Norman blinked, surprised by the gnome's fiery response. "I'm a *mighty* familiar, Yasmin. I am a *talking parrot*, not some run-of-the-mill crow!"

"Oh, please." Yasmin rolled her eyes. "You're a *familiar*, not a philosopher. If you were as clever as you claim, you wouldn't be acting like a child and dropping carrot peelings on our heads all evening."

"Norman," I admonished. "Did you do that?"

Annoyingly, he looked rather proud as he nodded his head yes.

Char gave him a stern look. "Where did you even get carrot peel from?" she asked and then quickly said, "Never mind. You must put a stop to this, Norman. You need to be the bigger—" she paused—"parrot, in this situation. Apologize to Yasmin or else I won't take you to the flower shop with me tomorrow, and you can stay here alone and think about your actions."

Norman squawked. "You didn't even wait to hear my side of the story." He flapped his wings. "We're supposed to be a team."

"Which is why I'm asking you nicely to get along with Yasmin. She shares our home and has as much of a right to be here as you," Char replied, both hands firmly planted on her hips.

"I'm *not* saying sorry," Norman said and then to my surprise he flew off in a huff.

We watched him go, and I turned to Char and said, "He'll be back soon, contrite no doubt. That little guy does have strong feelings."

"Tell me about it," Char said. Then she bent down to speak to Yasmin. "I'm sorry on his behalf. I'll keep on him to be more kind. We'll get through to him eventually."

Yasmin leaned over and hugged one of Char's ankles with her tiny arm. Those two were adorable.

Char put her key in the door and said she was off to have a bath. I asked her to make sure she double-locked the doors in her bedroom which led out to the patio and then wished her goodnight. "You did brilliantly this evening," I added. "We're all very proud."

Char blushed—a rare occurrence that usually only involved Owen Jones—and then mumbled 'thank you' before disappearing to her bedroom.

Smiling to myself, I climbed the stairs to my own bedroom, eager to find Blue and then crawl under the covers.

My familiar was already fast asleep, curled up on a fleece blanket at the foot of the bed. I gave her a little scratch behind the ears, then went to the window. The cloud had moved away from the face of the moon. Instead of closing the curtains, I opened the window to draw in a lungful of the full-moon air.

I breathed in the night air and could smell that rain was on its way. I tried to find my sense of peace but then I spied Norman in the distance, flapping his wings manically in a parrot huff. Beyond him was the spire of the church, and beyond that I knew was Fitzlupin Castle. I stared in its direction, again filled with an aching desire to see Alex. I just couldn't get used to him being locked away, even though I knew it was for his own physical good—and the good of those around him. Instead, I wanted his comfort and the distraction from my own thoughts, which were still plagued by my mom's message that something evil was in the air. These warnings tormented me because I couldn't put a name or a face to them. Instead I was left to imagine the worst.

I sighed, closed the window and drew the curtains.

By the time I got into bed it was well past midnight and, drawing Blue close to me, I laid my head on the cool pillow and waited for sleep to come.

Chapter Thirteen

On Sunday morning, I woke with a start, the remnants of bad dreams still clinging to my thoughts like cobwebs. The dreams had been twisted, full of whispering voices and shifting shapes that all turned into strange incarnations of roses, some dripping with tears, others with blood. It felt like something was waiting—watching, perhaps, just beyond the veil.

I blinked a few times, trying to come back to this world. I'd heard rain in the night, but this morning my bedroom was flooded with golden sunlight. Still, the atmosphere felt too thick, too suffocating, as if the shadows themselves were pressing down on me. I could still feel the echoes of fear that had chased me through the night, so I sat up slowly, the weight of my mom's warning still on my chest.

I rubbed my eyes, pushing the images away. I reached out for Blue, who was sound asleep. Her soft, ginger fur felt warm beneath my fingers, and she purred languidly, opening her eyes to stare into mine. "Good morning," I murmured, and she yawned before rearing back on her haunches to stretch. She sent me an inquiring look, picking up on my nervous energy, but I told her not to worry. The morning sun filtered through the gaps in the curtains in a golden beam. I let myself breathe and banished bad thoughts. It was seven a.m. Today was a new day, and although I was exhausted from a restless night, I had to bring my best and brightest self to the final day of the flower-arranging course.

After a quick shower, I stared at my wardrobe, looking for something to perk up my mood. My eyes lighted on an old floral dress, cream with pink roses. It was girlier than my usual style, so I didn't reach for it often, but since today had somehow become bridal bouquet day, it seemed fitting. I pulled it on, added a cropped cream cardigan, pinned my hair into a high bun and then added some small gold hoops to finish the look.

After coffee and a quick oatmeal breakfast, I left the still-sleeping farmhouse and headed out to pick up Imogen and some more supplies from Bewitching Blooms.

The sun was so bright I pulled on my sunglasses as I slid behind the wheel and eased my Range Rover onto the quiet village road. I drove slowly, my tires humming gently on the smooth, narrow lane. The sun was climbing higher now, casting long shadows across the fields and spilling light over the undulating hills that rolled away in the distance. I slowed as I passed the old mill, its wheel turning gently in the stream that ran beside it. The sound of water trickling over stone was soothing, almost hypnotic. I loved this time of day, the fields sparkling with dew-covered grass, the early risers out walking their dogs. I couldn't help but notice how peaceful everything seemed—no hurry, no rush. I tried to hold on to this new-day feeling and release the lingering worry of my dreams, which still clung to me.

Imogen was waiting outside, engrossed in something on her phone. She slipped into the passenger seat and said, "Beautiful morning," and I had to agree.

"Enjoy your Saturday night?" I asked.

She gave me a coy grin, unwilling to spill the details. "You?"

I grinned back. I couldn't share the events of my coven meeting either.

We stopped at Bewitching Blooms for more white roses, greenery, and floral foam and then drove back to the Tudor Rose.

The inn's terrace was already busy with the breakfast crowd but there was something unsettling about the scene that greeted me. The air, which had been fresh and clean on the drive in, now felt heavier, as if something lingered just beneath the surface. I could sense it the moment I stepped out of the car—a subtle but unnerving humming that seemed to hang like a cloak around the inn. I glanced at Imogen but she was busy unloading the flowers.

Feeling certain I was still unnerved by Mom's warning and the bad dreams that had followed, I tried to ignore the trepidation I felt and to focus on the day ahead. Our arms laden with buckets of flowers, we carefully made our way through the narrow corridors to the Damask Room. The curtains had already been pulled back and the room was glowing with sunshine. Imogen worked quickly and efficiently and together we readied the room for another day of teaching.

Frederick was the first to arrive. He was beaming and

greeted us both with dramatic air kisses. "Darlings," he said, "I owe you both a huge 'thank you.' I presented my arrangement to Roberto last night and he was delighted with the surprise. In fact, he's planning a dinner party simply so I can show off my new talent." Quickly he added, "If that isn't too boastful to say."

"Not at all." I laughed. "You're a natural. I thought your bouquet was quite spectacular."

"As did I," a honied voice chimed in.

I turned to see Gillian Fairfax enter the room. If it was possible, she looked even more beautiful than normal. Her golden hair was pinned away from her face and flowed down her back. She was wearing a pair of gray silk slacks and matching shirt, which brought out the silvery tones of her pale eyes. Her skin shone and her eyelids glistened with a subtle shimmer. Once again, her outfit was completely inappropriate for the activity, but she did look gorgeous.

She embraced Frederick, who clasped her hands in his. "Peony, Imogen, and Gillian, I would adore for you to be the first guests I invite to our dinner party. I can't think of a more beautiful trio."

Gillian smiled. "You flatter us, my dear," she said, but softly touched her hair making sure there wasn't a strand out of place.

"I'm afraid I'm with Frederick on this one," another voice said. It was Lucas, who entered the room with a broad smile. He, too, was carefully dressed in dark slacks and a pressed white linen shirt that matched the pearliness of his perfect teeth.

Frederick reached out to clasp Lucas's hand as he passed

their table and said, "I'd invite you, too, only it's a long way to come."

"It's only a short journey from London," Lucas replied. "I'd be delighted to come to your party." As he spoke, Lucas glanced at Gillian, taking in her appearance as one might a beautiful painting.

There was such sincerity in his admiring look that I couldn't help but root for Lucas. Of course, Gillian obviously noticed the pointed look—Lucas would make the drive from London back to the Cotswolds to see *her*—but she was playing it cool. Very cool. The way that woman handled men was an artform.

The rest of the group began to drift in, first Jo and Helena, then the Hildebrands. At five past ten, Arabella and Verity arrived, the daughter yawning.

I glanced at my watch again, eager to start the morning session, but we were still missing Tamsin.

Verity yawned again, loudly this time, and her mother admonished her. "Honestly, darling, do cover your mouth when you yawn."

Verity rolled her eyes at her mom and then apologized. "Hugo and I were up far too late last night," she said, now smiling. "We were the last to leave the dining room. Dinner was simply delicious, then we drank whiskey cocktails and stayed up talking into the night. It was lovely to have time with just the two of us. We seem to do everything as a foursome, not that I'm complaining, of course. Tamsin's my best friend and Jasper is Hugo's, but sometimes it's nice just to be a couple."

Although she wasn't looking in her mother's direction, I felt the comment was pointed.

Arabella said, "And I was perfectly happy with room service." Her tone was bright and breezy but I could see she didn't mean it.

"As was Tamsin," Arabella continued. "She was tired, too, and also ordered room service." In a conspiratorial voice she added, "I think she hoped Jasper would make it back last night and was waiting to be surprised."

Verity shook her head. "Hugo said the meeting went late. Jasper stayed in town."

"Shame," said Arabella. "I'm sure those two could have done with some alone time, as well."

I swallowed. Only I knew how loaded this comment was. I checked my watch again. It was ten minutes past ten. "Let's get started," I said brightly. "I'm sure Tamsin will be down shortly."

Verity frowned. "It's not like Tamsin to sleep in. She's up early like clockwork every day. It's a hangover from her intensive training days. That girl doesn't know how to relax. I'll give her a call."

She picked up her phone, made the call, and then frowned. "There's no answer."

"Maybe she's on the phone to her agent again," Arabella suggested. "Go and tell her to come down, Vee." There was irritation in the tone. Verity looked as though she'd argue and then thought better of it.

I could sense the rest of the room was itching to get started, unbothered by the late arrival of the group's least enthusiastic member, but Verity said she'd quickly run up to the suite they were sharing and remind Tamsin that we were starting.

She said, "Her head has been all over the place what with

new work negotiations and her paranoia about the stalker's release." She excused herself.

"Do you think we might be able to get started without them?" Kent asked.

Arabella frowned but I thought it would be a good idea to talk through the day's proceedings and then Arabella could catch the two women up. I took my position at the front of the room, feeling the buzz of anticipation as the group's focus turned to me. I took a deep breath. "All right, everyone," I began, my voice steady but warm, "today we're going to create a formal arrangement, with an extra focus on bridal flowers for those who are interested."

Helena and Arabella beamed.

"It's going to be more complex than yesterday," I continued, "but I promise you, once you break it down step by step, it'll make sense."

I laid out the materials on the table—long, elegant stems of roses, lilies, orchids, and a mix of greenery. The first thing I explained was the importance of balance and proportion. "In formal arrangements, symmetry is key," I said, picking up a few stems of the tallest flowers. I was about to continue when the door flew open with a bang.

It was Verity. She was white and shaking.

"What is it?" I asked, alarm spreading through me like wildfire.

She stared at me, aghast. Trembling, she said, "I don't know what to do. It's Tamsin. I found... She..."

With a moan she fell to the floor.

"My God, she's fainted," Frederick cried out.

Arabella leapt from her seat and rushed towards her daughter. The room was suddenly a flurry of activity.

"Call 999," Jo shouted.

"Give her some space," Grace said. "She's simply fainted. She needs air."

"She needs water," Lucas said.

"Or smelling salts," Jo added. "Does anyone have smelling salts?"

"My darling," Frederick said, "It's not the 1900s. No one carries smelling salts in their handbags."

"Can everyone please shut up," Arabella said. She was crouched over her daughter, stroking her face. "She's coming to." Arabella looked up at me and said, "Peony, can you go and see what's wrong with Tamsin?" She picked up the keycard from where Verity had dropped it. "They're in the Princess Elizabeth suite, second floor at the end of the hallway."

I nodded and took the keycard from her outstretched hand. I was filled with dread, certain that Jessie Rae's warning, my terrible dreams, and this morning's sense of unease as I arrived at the inn were all adding up to this moment. Something terrible had happened here in the night. And I was about to discover what.

I ran up the creaking stairs, my heart pounding and blood thumping in my ears. The hallway at the top was dim, lit only by a weak strip of sunlight slanting in from a nearby window. It felt colder here and as I drew closer to the suite a terrible tremor shook my body and then I knew for certain what lay on the other side.

Death.

I put the keycard to the door and felt a jolt as it beeped. I called out Tamsin's name.

There was no answer. Of course, there was no answer.

I stood for a moment, listening to the terrible pulse of the silence, then walked into the suite. The living room was spacious and inviting, with old oak beams criss-crossing the ceiling, and furnished with plush velvet sofas in deep emerald and gold. A large stone fireplace dominated one wall, its mantel adorned with antique brass candelabras; in front of it an ornate rug with rich reds and blues softened the hardwood floors. I spotted Verity's bouquet from yesterday on the coffee table. Everything about the room was luxurious and cozy but I knew something awful had happened here. There was a small kitchenette and a pair of doors which led to the two adjoining bedrooms. I didn't have to guess which was Tamsin's. I felt the darkness pulling me in.

I slowly went towards it. I took a shaky breath and opened the door.

The curtains were drawn and the room was dimly lit, the only light cast by two vintage-style sconces mounted on the walls which threw distorted shadows across the floor. The room was still, too still, the air thick with the pungent scent of flowers.

I took another step forward.

In the center of the bedroom was a king-sized bed draped in luxurious linens—thick, creamy white duvets layered with plush pillows in shades of soft lavender and gold. And that's where she lay.

I froze.

"Tamsin," I whispered again.

Silence.

"Tamsin?"

I went towards the bed, holding my breath, still drawn towards it as by a magnetic force.

Tamsin's body was on top of the sheets, sheathed in a beautiful cream silk nightdress—the kind of gown that a woman wears when she's expecting a man to visit. She was surrounded by roses, the petals wilted and browned at the edges.

There was no life left here. She was dead.

I backed away.

It was a terrible sight. Like an effigy which had been left to wither and rot. I looked across to the dresser and saw the vase which had held Tamsin's bouquet. Someone had removed all the roses, leaving behind only the green stems.

I shuddered again, feeling a swirl of turbulence surrounding the body. And then I noticed one of the bed's pillows on the floor. A chill went through me. I looked closely at Tamsin's face. There was no sign of suffocation, but I got the sense that Tamsin had died because that very pillow had been held over her face.

Had she worn that lovely gown for a man?

But which man was she expecting?

And could that have something to do with her death?

Chapter Fourteen

I was still standing over Tamsin's body when there was a knock on the outer door. It was a nervous, timid sound but it ripped through me, jarring my nerves. I left the bedroom and went to see who was waiting on the other side.

I opened the door to reveal a young woman in a smart chambermaid's uniform. She was holding a pile of fresh linen and a cleaning cart sat against the wall behind her. "I'm sorry to disturb you," she said, her tone even and filled with a practiced kind of politeness. "I'll come back later."

The girl couldn't have been more than nineteen, with a slender but sturdy build and dark hair tied in a neat ponytail. Her eyes were bright and green, with a keenness to them that suggested she was always observing and attentive to the needs of the guests.

I needed to get back downstairs. Stupidly, I'd rushed up without pausing to grab my phone. When I asked the young woman if she had her phone with her, she looked a bit nervous, but nodded. I told her to call the police and tell them someone had died in that room, then to remain where she was, but on no account was she to enter that room or let anyone but the police enter it. Did she understand? She gulped and said she did. I waited until she got out her phone and then headed back downstairs. Behind me I heard her say, "Sophia, it's Millie from housekeeping." The maid wasn't calling the police, but her boss. I suppose if I'd been in her position I'd have done the same thing.

When I got downstairs, Sophia met me. "Peony," she said softly, pulling me into a quiet corner. "What's happened?"

Quickly I explained. She grew pale, but had obviously dealt with crises before. She told me she'd phone the police and would personally stand guard outside Tamsin's suite to make sure no one went in.

"That includes Hugo, Verity, and Jasper, should he show up."

"Yes. Of course." She obviously knew her business so I told her I was going to go back to the Damask Room. "It was Verity Ainsworth who found her first. We'll wait there, as the police will want us to give statements."

Sophia called the police even as she headed up the stairs. Me? I took a beat. I was in no rush to return to the Damask Room. My mind was still processing the awful bedroom scene. Tamsin's pale, prostrate body. The terrible browning roses and the smell of decay which permeated the room. And then there was that darkness, how it had sucked me in, pulled me into its midst. I'd sensed from the second I'd entered the suite that evil lurked there. I tried to cleanse my mind and refocus it on what had to be done next. I needed to stay calm and practical. The first thing was to reassure the group and make sure we all stayed in one place. By now, I knew the ways of the police and that they would want to speak to everyone who had seen Tamsin yesterday.

But when I entered the Damask Room, it was a scene of emotional chaos.

Verity was sobbing hysterically, Arabella's arms around her. The others looked terrified and in various states of shock. Jo was saying, "I just can't believe it. I can't believe it." And Frederick was murmuring something about Tamsin's vitality. They were all talking over each other, some demanding answers, wanting to know why and how this could have happened.

When I walked in, everyone turned to me except Verity, who was still crying hysterically. Over her head, Arabella sent me a questioning glance and I nodded. Verity must have come to and told the room that her best friend was dead. And now I'd confirmed the fact to Verity's mother, who closed her eyes in pain.

To the room at large I stuck to the simplest facts I could. I said Tamsin was dead and the police had been sent for.

"But she was so alive just yesterday," Jo said, sounding as though she didn't believe me. "Whatever happened to her?"

"Could have been a heart attack. It happens sometimes to athletes, even young ones." This was Helena. I could have told her Tamsin hadn't died of a heart attack, but I held my peace.

"Or an aneurysm," Jo added. "My second cousin died of a brain aneurysm. He wasn't even forty. Just dropped dead."

After casting a glance at the two women who seemed to be going over every sudden death they'd ever heard of, the Hildebrands came forward. "Is there anything we can do?"

"I don't think so." I explained that the manager had

alerted the police and was making sure no one went into the room. Then Sophia came in. As she passed me, she said softly, "I've put a security guard outside the door."

Before my grateful eyes, Sophia took control of the room. She must have witnessed all sorts of chaos at the inn over the years. She didn't let her own emotions slip past her professional mask, but I could see the tension in her jaw, hear the way her voice cracked slightly when she spoke.

"Please," she said, her voice calm but firm, trying to cut through everyone talking at once. "I know you're all in shock, and I understand this is very difficult for you all. But right now, we need to stay calm. The police are on their way. We're going to get to the bottom of what happened here."

The room quietened a little, though it was clear they were still reeling. Sophia kept her gaze steady, moving from one person to the next, her eyes locking with theirs in a way that was both soothing and commanding. I could see her trying to pull them back from the edge of panic, offering them a small anchor in the midst of the storm.

Verity let out another terrible sob and I went to her then, placing a hand on her shoulder. "I know," I whispered. "I know. It's awful. But we'll get through this, I promise."

I let Sophia continue to calm the other guests, guiding them through their confusion and fear. Soon, the sound of sirens filled the air. I went to the window and saw an ambulance pull up outside and paramedics rush out. I swallowed. If only their skills could save Tamsin, but she was gone.

Next, four police officers in uniforms exited the wailing cars. Just behind them was a dark Mercedes, which I knew belonged to Detective Inspector Michelle Rawlins. Sure enough, the passenger's door opened and a polished pair of brown shoes emerged, followed by the rest of DI Rawlins. She cut an impressive figure in her navy suit and short gray hair. Her partner, Sergeant Dwight Evans, emerged from the driver's side. He was perhaps ten years younger than his boss, although I had always found him to be impressively mature and capable. Plus, there was something mischievous behind his dark eyes which made him warmer, and more approachable than DI Rawlins. I knew that the crime investigation team would soon arrive.

Sophia excused herself to speak with the police. At the door, she paused and said, "I'll have some coffee brought in." She shot a final glance at Verity, who was still sobbing in her mother's arms. I could tell she was thinking that Verity might need something stronger.

Since Sophia had told everyone all we knew so far, I knew my job now was to keep the group in the room. When the coffee and tea arrived, Imogen leapt to her feet and together we began to pour cups of hot, strong coffee and pass them around. I whispered a quick spell of calm over Verity's and sweetened it with a little sugar to revive her nerves. The poor girl was still trembling.

Suddenly, I felt a strong sense of something good arriving —like a cool balm smoothed across hot skin. I continued to hand out coffees, but now I felt like everything really was under control.

If someone had asked me, I wouldn't have been able to say why, but then a few moments later, it all made sense.

Alex burst into the room, out of breath and looking frantic. When his pale eyes lighted on mine, his face flooded with relief. "Peony," he said and rushed over to where I was handing Gillian a coffee. "I'm so glad to see that you're safe."

Gillian looked surprised but said nothing. Instead, she excused herself and crossed the room to where Frederick was conversing with Jo.

Alex hugged me, something we had not yet done in public, and then growled in my ear, "I sensed trouble close to you and was losing my mind not being able to get to you." He pulled away then and looked me deeply in the eyes. "I was frantic."

"I know," I whispered. "I tried to send you a message last night that I was nearby."

"I felt it. But I also felt a darkness coming from the heart of the village and somehow I knew you were close to it. What's happened here?"

"Tamsin Mortimer is dead. It looks like she was murdered."

Alex's brow furrowed. "Tamsin Mortimer? The woman we saw at lunch on Friday?"

I nodded grimly. "The very same. She was on my flower arranging course with her best friend." I gestured over at the still-sobbing Verity.

Alex gripped my hands tightly and I looked down. His fingers were red and raw, his palms covered in scratches. I exclaimed, "You look like you've been in a fight!"

"I was trying to get out of the castle dungeon. I was so desperate to get to you."

I touched his hands again, turning the palms over in mine. Quietly, I said, "Come home with me tonight and I'll put some magic salve on those wounds. They'll heal right up."

He smiled and stroked the inside of my palm. I sat him

down and poured him a hot coffee and then one for myself. Goodness knows I needed it.

A moment later, the atmosphere in the room suddenly changed and everyone quietened down. I looked up to see Detective Inspector Rawlins and Sergeant Evans in the doorway. It was amazing how quickly everyone responded to their authority.

DI Rawlins spoke first. She introduced herself and then Sergeant Evans. I couldn't believe I was back in the company of a couple of murder detectives. She asked all of us to tell her and the sergeant anything we could about the death of Tamsin Mortimer.

A ripple went through the room at the word *death*.

Jo sucked in a startled breath and cried, "Was Tamsin *murdered*?!" She'd obviously just realized that detectives probably wouldn't interview us if Tamsin had died of natural causes.

"We're treating her death as suspicious, ma'am. We'd be very grateful if you could help with our inquiries."

"Are we suspects?" Helena asked. If I'm honest, she sounded quite pleased at being a suspect, as though she were starring in an episode of Midsomer Murders.

"No. But each of you could shed light on Tamsin Mortimer's final hours."

From there Sergeant Evans took over, taking out a notebook and pen. I watched as the sergeant moved around the room, asking everyone's name, his slightly scuffed brogues making a steady, methodical sound on the wooden floor. He paused in front of Verity and Arabella. I could see he was making a mental note to come to them last, once Verity had calmed down.

When he asked Alex to say his name, Alex gave his full title, something he almost never did. Evans paused, obviously recognizing him, while the flower arrangers–the ones who didn't already know who Alex was–glanced over. No matter what you see on British TV, most of us don't come across lords in real life. In Alex's loftiest lord-of-the-manor tone, he explained that he wasn't part of the flower-arranging course but had come to see me this morning. I tried my best not to blush.

With all names, notes, and everyone's contact information gathered, DI Rawlins asked if we could pool our knowledge of Tamsin's last day and evening. She said they'd ask each of us to state what we knew of the deceased and when we'd last seen her.

It was casual enough, and to a certain extent, everyone in the room relaxed.

DI Rawlins looked at Frederick, who had the awkward task of being the first to speak. He considered for a moment, pulling his beard with one hand, then said he'd followed Tamsin Mortimer's tennis career and enjoyed watching her when she was a contestant on British Ballroom. He mentioned that she'd rushed out of the room at the end of the afternoon to take a call. "I had dinner at home with my husband, Roberto," he said, "and then we stayed in for the rest of the night. I drove back here this morning."

"And you'd never met Ms. Mortimer before yesterday?" DI Rawlins asked him, her words casual, but her gaze sharp.

Frederick pulled at his beard again, as the silence lengthened. Finally, he said, "I wrote to her when she was a dance contestant. She was so alive, so..." He seemed to be having trouble coming up with the right word and then said, "Wonderful. I found I wanted to paint her. I rarely paint people, but I felt inspired. She agreed to meet with me, but, in the end, nothing came of it."

His words grew terse.

"You decided you didn't want to paint her?" DI Rawlins pressed.

"She decided she didn't have time," Frederick admitted.

"You must have been very disappointed."

He appeared alarmed. "Not disappointed enough to kill her, if that's what you mean."

"Did she seem pleased to see you again?" DI Rawlins continued as though he hadn't spoken.

"I don't think she remembered me," he said, sounding irritable.

"Did you renew your offer to paint her?" the sergeant asked.

"I was thinking about it," Frederick admitted. "Something about her made my fingers itch for a paintbrush."

And yet he'd never said a word to any of us about knowing her before. I was surprised and had to wonder what other secrets Frederick might be keeping.

They moved on and, in that way, they worked their way round the rest of the group.

The room smelled faintly of flowers, but there was an underlying tension, a heaviness that didn't belong in a place like this. I looked around and caught Imogen's eye. The color had drained from her face and in her hands was a wheel of pale pink satin ribbon, which she turned over and over, unconsciously. Next to her were several buckets of flowers which we had so carefully prepared, and all the necessary accessories laid out in neat rows, ready to be distributed to each attendee. Imogen had gone to great lengths to source some extra bridal bits at the last minute. The care and thought which had gone into this day now seemed so very sad. I tried to give her a reassuring look but I knew that it would take so much more for anyone to feel better today.

The detectives asked us where we'd been last night. Imogen said she'd gone home, had a bath and slept deeply as she was so tired from teaching all day. I was slightly less forthcoming for obvious reasons. I said I'd spent the evening with a group of friends, which was true enough. The other witches were my friends. Sisters even. And in one case, a mother.

Rawlins and Evans continued to question the room. The sergeant's questions were always the same, but each answer was different. Each of us had been touched by Tamsin in some way; we all had memories of Tamsin—of something she'd said or something we'd witnessed. I knew that these observations would help in the end, but it was difficult to imagine how we might help the detectives catch her murderer.

Helena looked especially frightened and Jo squeezed her hand. They left together. Gillian, whose life had been touched by death recently, seemed the most calm, answering DI Rawlins's questions in a clear, thoughtful tone, explaining that she had honestly paid Tamsin very little attention and she, too, hadn't seen her since the end of the course.

DI Rawlins finally came to Verity, who was gripping her mother's hand. Arabella was also clearly upset but trying to hold it together for the sake of her daughter.

Rawlins said, "The hotel manager told us you were sharing a suite with Tamsin Mortimer and her husband,

Jasper Faringdon. So, you may have been the last person to see Tamsin alive," she said. "Please try to remember every detail of the evening. Even the things which seem inconsequential can help us piece together her last hours."

Verity's face was pale, her mouth still trembling. "Mummy, do I have to?" she wailed, sounding like a child.

"You must be brave, darling. Tamsin deserves our help. It's the last thing we can do for her." Arabella's voice trembled.

Verity said, "But it's all so awful. I was right there, in the suite, when she...when she..." And she began to cry. But through her tears, she began telling us that Tamsin had been annoyed that Jasper had to go to London. Verity had assured her that she was welcome to join Hugo and her for dinner, butTamsin had said she was certain they'd rather dine alone than as a threesome.

She wiped her wet eyes with the back of her hand and glanced around the room with a look of despair. "And the truth is, she was right. She was my best friend and on her last night on earth I let her order room service so I could have my fiancé to myself."

I couldn't help a glance at Arabella. It was such an interesting choice of words. 'So I could have my fiancé to myself.' Had Verity known all along that her fiancé and best friend were having an affair? Worse, had she decided to end the affair permanently?

The roses circling Tamsin's body seemed to me to be giving a strong signal of twisted love or love gone wrong. Why else had the killer arranged the roses around her in that macabre way?

Then Arabella said, as though to soothe her daughter,

"But Tamsin was probably happy to spend an evening in her suite so she could work out the details of the new TV job her agent had told her about." Then Arabella explained about the possibility of her becoming an expert commentator for women's tennis. "It was an excellent opportunity for her," Arabella said, and I could see the successful executive in her and understood how she'd seen that same quality of ambition in her daughter's friend.

I felt as though a cloud were descending–a dark, heavy thing–then faint noises from outside made me realize they were moving the body. While we'd been in this room, the forensic team and all the other experts associated with a murder scene had been upstairs collecting physical clues while the two detectives were with those of us who'd been with Tamsin on her last day.

Verity started speaking again, more calmly now. "After dinner, Hugo, my fiancé, and I came back to the suite. We had drunk a little bit so we went straight to our bedroom." She paused. "How did I not hear something? I let her down. She was my best friend."

"It's not your fault," Arabella whispered. "You couldn't have known."

Verity began to cry again and the room shifted. I realized everyone was watching her intently.

"And did you—"

She was interrupted by the door opening, and in walked Hugo. He was wearing running gear and his cheeks had a healthy red glow. I don't know how, but he managed to look fresh and handsome despite clearly having been on a long run. Maybe he was one of those rare and lucky guys who never broke a sweat, no matter what they did. The easy smile fell from his face when he saw Verity, and then that red glow all but disappeared when he took in the two detectives. "What's going on?" he asked quickly. "I got a call from Arabella to come back to the hotel immediately." He frowned. "Has someone been robbed? Verity, is it your engagement ring?"

Verity leapt to her feet and threw herself on his chest. "Tamsin is dead," she cried out.

He pulled away immediately and held Verity away from him, staring down at her. "What on earth do you mean?"

"She's dead! I found her on the bed upstairs. It was...it was unspeakable. I can't. Oh, Hugo." She pressed her face into his chest again, sobbing.

"It can't be so," Hugo murmured. He looked at Arabella, who nodded grimly. The tension between the two of them was palpable. I wondered if Hugo knew that Arabella was aware of his indiscretion. No doubt Tamsin had told him.

Hugo looked ill. "What happened to her? I don't understand. We were right next door. How could one of our dearest friends have died without us knowing anything about it?"

My skin prickled as he said the word 'friend' and I could see Arabella was inwardly reeling.

He pried Verity from his chest and insisted on getting her a glass of water. Imogen leapt into action and poured him one, then he took a seat next to his fiancée and Arabella. I shuddered as I realized he was unconsciously sitting in the same chair Tamsin had occupied.

Chapter Fifteen

"I'm sorry, Miss Ainsworth," DI Rawlins said, "I know this is very difficult for you, but we haven't finished with our questions. Now your fiancé is also here, he might be able to help us too."

Hugo audibly swallowed but said he would be happy to help get to the bottom of this awful turn of events.

Verity drained her glass of water and looked up at the detective. Her eyes were red and puffy, black mascara running in rivulets down her flushed cheeks. She nodded and DI Rawlins took her cue to continue.

"We know that Tamsin Mortimer ate dinner in her room. The manager personally brought up her tray around eight p.m. yesterday evening. Did you see or hear anything when you returned to the suite after dinner?"

Verity shook her head, then turned to Hugo. "We got back around eleven p.m., right?"

He nodded. "I think so. We'd had a little to drink. Cocktails and wine, you know."

DI Rawlins did not comment. But I couldn't help but

wonder if this detail made Verity and Hugo unreliable witnesses.

"And you say you heard no sound coming from her room at all?" DI Rawlins continued.

"No. The light in her room was out. I remember checking because Tamsin is the kind of person who needs her sleep, you know, and I didn't want us to disturb her when we came in. When I saw the light was off, I didn't want to risk waking her to say goodnight." She wiped her eyes again. "How I wish I had."

Sophia had been listening. She spoke up then. "If you didn't speak to her after dinner, then I must be the last person she spoke to. Apart from..." She left the ending of that sentence hanging.

"Oh, no, wait," she said, all of a fluster. "I remember now that Tamsin was on her phone when I brought up the tray. She was typing furiously. She seemed pretty upset. It's part of my job to mind my business and be discreet, so I pushed the matter out of my mind. But it means I wasn't the last to speak to her, if you count messaging."

DI Rawlins's focus sharpened. "You're certain she was on her phone?"

"Absolutely. She nodded when I brought in the tray, but was completely focused on her phone."

I hadn't spent a long time in Tamsin's room, but I'd done a slow, visual sweep, trying to gather any information I could from the room where Tamsin Mortimer had died. I was positive I had not seen a phone.

DI Rawlins asked, "Did anyone else have a keycard to the room?"

"Jasper, of course," Hugo replied. "Though he's taken it to London with him. And Arabella."

At this, I came forward and handed back Verity's keycard, which Arabella had given to me earlier.

"Your mother had a key to your room?" DI Rawlins asked.

Arabella nodded. "Verity lost hers almost as soon as we checked in. She's like that, I'm afraid. She made the hotel give her a new keycard, but when she found the original under her bed later that day she told me to keep it in case she lost hers again."

At this, Sophia frowned. Verity had clearly caused a nuisance with the lost card and perhaps even broken a hotel rule by sharing it with her mother. And so now we knew that Arabella had had access to the suite.

"When is Mr. Faringdon expected to return from London?" Rawlins asked, directing the question at Hugo.

But it was Arabella who answered. "I called him earlier and he's already on the road." In a quieter voice she said, "I explained there was an emergency and he was needed back immediately. I didn't want to tell him over the phone." She swallowed hard. "I couldn't."

DI Rawlins simply nodded. It was as if the group were held under the spell of her authority—a natural magic which I was certain DI Rawlins didn't know she possessed.

The Hildebrands had stayed in a room on the floor above the Princess Elizabeth suite.

"We didn't see or hear anything," Kent said, running a hand through his gray hair.

Grace looked less sure. DI Rawlins noticed this immediately. She turned to Kent's wife and asked, "Perhaps there's something coming to mind?"

Grace looked nervous. Very nervous. "I didn't close our curtains properly last night and the light came in and woke me up. I went to the window and when I looked out, the garden was so pretty by moonlight I stayed there a while. It was a full moon, you see, and so beautiful."

I felt like we were all waiting for Grace to continue.

"And, well." She hesitated. "I saw a young couple kissing in the moonlight. It was very romantic. But I didn't see their faces."

The room drew a collective breath. Who was outside kissing?

Sergeant Evans asked, "What time was this?"

"A little after midnight."

Now everyone in the room turned to look at Hugo and Verity.

Verity, who had finally stopped sobbing, said, "It wasn't us. I told you already. We went to bed at eleven p.m."

Grace added, "I saw a light go on and off again about the same time. It was the floor below us. I think it was your suite."

Verity said, "Maybe that was you going to the toilet, Hugo."

Hugo looked startled. "I beg your pardon?"

Verity replied, "You woke me when you got out of bed. And you were gone ages."

Hugo looked aghast. All the earlier rosiness had gone from his cheeks and now he looked decidedly unwell. Verity was probably in too much shock to realize that her throw-away comment now cast Hugo in a suspicious light.

Hugo let go of Verity's hand and wrapped his arms around his stomach. "I was having tummy trouble," he said, avoiding looking anyone in the eye.

Now my own stomach began to churn, feeling the pieces of Grace's and Verity's stories align. I had the feeling that if Verity kept talking, she was going to get her fiancé into some very hot water. And likely get her own heart trampled on in the process.

DI Rawlins kept her gaze level and directed at Verity—who still seemed clueless as to what was happening.

"Miss Ainsworth," DI Rawlins asked, "what time was this?"

"It was exactly twelve-fifteen. I glanced at the clock."

"And what time did Hugo come back to bed?"

Suddenly Verity looked frightened. Her eyes widened and began to fill with tears. "I don't know," she stumbled. "Not long, I suppose. Ten minutes. Maybe five."

It was obvious that Verity was lying. And if I could see it, so could the sharp and experienced eye of Michelle Rawlins. In a considered tone, she asked, "If that is the case, then who was the couple in the garden?"

Silence filled the room. It was thick and heavy and I suddenly felt the need to open a window. I looked around the room and saw that most of the group had found something to fiddle with. Imogen was twisting a piece of vine; Gillian was playing with an earring; Jo and Helena were shuffling their notebooks; Lucas was clicking the lid of his pen. Only Alex remained completely still. I felt oddly proud of his composure. I felt that I could rely on him in any situation.

The silence went on.

And on.

And yet DI Rawlins said nothing. She waited. And waited. Clearly her instinct was that someone here knew something and was about to crack.

Finally, Lucas cleared his throat. "Um," he said, "the couple in the garden was Gillian and me." He paused, and then turned to look at Gillian. She was blushing and looked extremely awkward. Lucas continued, "I'm so sorry, Gillian. This is very ungentlemanly of me, but it very much seems like this is turning into a murder investigation. I have to be truthful and clear up this matter."

Gillian gave a small, affirmative nod.

But then Grace, quite charmingly, raised her hand as if she was in a school classroom. "Excuse me, I don't want to complicate matters, but Lucas wasn't the man I saw in the garden."

DI Rawlins spun on her heels and looked at Grace inquisitively. "I thought you couldn't make out the identity of the couple?"

Grace gulped but I could tell she was trying to hold her own in this unnerving space. "No, I couldn't see any faces but I did see their silhouettes. The man's hair was full and slightly wavy. Lucas's hair is short. It wasn't him. I'm certain of it."

All eyes went to Hugo, who was now self-consciously touching his thick, lustrous hair.

"Yes," Grace said quietly. "Like Hugo's."

Verity leaned away from Hugo and stared at him as though he were a monster.

In that moment, I felt as convinced as I'd ever been of anything that Verity had known perfectly well that her fiancé and best friend were involved.

DI Rawlins addressed the group and said that Alex, Jo, Helena, and Frederick were free to go.

I apologized to the three of them for the course being so

tragically ended. Jo and Helena couldn't get out of the room fast enough, but Frederick came to thank me. "I learned so much, Peony, thank you. And I look forward to doing this again sometime."

He said a quick goodbye to Gillian and then left.

Alex looked at me, obviously reluctant to go. I told him not to worry, to return home, and I'd call him as soon as I could. I would have loved Alex to stay by my side, but the last thing he needed was to become embroiled in a murder investigation. He gave my arm a quick squeeze and then left.

Now DI Rawlins returned to Gillian and Lucas.

"Did either of you see or hear anything while you were in the garden last night?"

Lucas shook his head. "I was focused on Gillian. I don't remember seeing anyone else."

Gillian blushed. But she also looked less certain. Quietly she said, "Lucas and I had dinner at a restaurant nearby and then came back to the hotel so I could pick up my car. We walked for a while in the garden, the moonlight *was* very pretty last night. And that's when I thought I heard low voices talking. It might have been paranoia, since I didn't want to be seen—because of privacy, you understand—so I suggested to Lucas that we go back inside. We had a nightcap and then I drove home."

"Did you recognize the voices?" DI Rawlins asked.

Gillian shook her head. "They were just murmurs. I couldn't make out a distinct voice."

So, another couple were in the garden. Was it possible that it was Hugo and Tamsin? How long had Hugo really been out of bed?

"And what time did you arrive home?" Rawlins asked Gillian.

"A little after one a.m."

I was pleased that Gillian had allowed Lucas's obvious admiration to turn into something more. But this detail didn't bode well for Hugo. I shot a look in his direction. He was perspiring at the temples. So, a long run didn't make him break into sweat, but being questioned by the police, did. I felt torn. Obviously, the affair between Tamsin and Hugo was a vital piece of information in this investigation. But it wasn't up to me to upend Verity's life. I looked at Arabella. She was still as white as a sheet but decidedly quiet. I couldn't rely on her to tell the truth to the authorities. There was only one way forward: I would tell the detectives what I knew about Tamsin and Hugo's relationship. But in private.

Now Rawlins turned back to Hugo. "Did you often travel with Tamsin Mortimer and Jasper Faringdon?"

Hugo nodded, trying to arrange his features into a more relaxed expression. "Yes. We're all best friends. The women knew one another from school and Jasper and I are in business together. We often socialize together. I was best man at Jasper's wedding last year and he's set to be mine. Verity and I are tying the knot next summer."

"So you would say that you knew Ms. Mortimer and Mr. Faringdon very well," DI Rawlins asked.

Hugo nodded, like it was a stupid question.

"And theirs was a happy marriage?"

"Oh, yes," Verity answered, not giving Hugo a chance to answer.

But DI Rawlins kept her focus on Hugo. "And you are

business partners with Mr. Faringdon. How is the business doing?"

Hugo visibly relaxed. Clearly, this was a subject he felt comfortable with. "Extremely well," Hugo said. "In fact, we were written up in the Financial Times, Financiers Under Forty, as they like to call it. We run a hedge fund together. GoldenBridge."

DI Rawlins's gaze narrowed. She was watching Hugo very carefully, taking in each of his gestures, the small inflections as he spoke.

To Verity she said, "Do you know if your friend had life insurance?"

Verity looked shocked. "Goodness. I have no idea. I know she had all kinds of insurance while she was playing tennis professionally. I mean, her right hand was insured."

I swallowed. I didn't like where this was going. The ease which Hugo had affected just moments ago was gone. My mind began to work double-time. Hugo was clearly a man who came from money and loved money. He worked with it and he obviously enjoyed spending it. And he was having an affair that could have jeopardized his chances of marrying Verity. How much would the scandal hurt his business, his reputation and his future if the secret got out? I wondered if Tamsin had wanted more from Hugo. Perhaps she had begun to pressure him into telling Verity about their affair, perhaps even threatening to go public herself? Would this have been enough incentive for Hugo to kill his lover? All he had to do was walk across the living room to the other bedroom, smother Tamsin, and then slip back into his own bed again.

I studied Hugo, wondering if beyond the expensive

athletic leisure gear, there was a will strong enough to commit the most terrible of crimes.

DI Rawlins asked the question again, now directed at Hugo. He echoed back the question. "Did Tamsin have life insurance? Yes. Yes, she did. Five million." He said it matter-of-factly but DI Rawlins repeated, "Five million pounds?"

"That's right. The company pays for the policy. If Jasper died, Tamsin would get five million; if she died, he would get the same amount. Should I die, Verity is my beneficiary and as soon as we're married, she'll be added to the policy."

Arabella suddenly took her daughter's hand in hers.

DI Rawlins looked at the three of them. "Can any of you think of a reason why someone might murder Tamsin Mortimer?"

Each of them looked horrified. As I waited to hear their answer, my mother's words suddenly came into my head.

The rose is pretty...but beware its thorns.

Chapter Sixteen

Rawlins' terrible question remained unanswered because at that moment, Jasper Faringdon rushed into the room, his eyes searching the group wildly.

"What's going on?" he asked. "There are police everywhere. I can't get through to my wife. Where is she?"

Again, that awful silence. Jasper's dark hair was disheveled as though he'd been tugging at it the entire drive back to the Cotswolds. He was dressed in expensive-looking jeans, a crisp navy polo shirt, and navy sports jacket with brown loafers. I noticed these details with some surprise, as I'd expected him to have come straight from meetings.

Arabella stood up. "Jasper," she said softly, "I am so sorry. Tamsin, she's been found dead." She went to him, trying to pull him into an embrace, but he jumped back.

"What are you talking about? I saw her just yesterday. She was arranging flowers."

DI Rawlins cleared her throat and introduced herself. "Jasper Faringdon?"

Jasper nodded.

DI Rawlins said, "I'm afraid what Mrs. Ainsworth says is true. Your wife is dead. I'm very sorry for your loss."

There was a gruff kindness to DI Rawlins's words and I imagined this was one of the worst parts of her job, telling people that their loved ones were dead.

Jasper's face was still drawn in confusion, like he couldn't quite piece together what he was hearing. His eyes were wide and blank and they flickered between the lead detective to Verity, and then settled on the window behind her head. His face began to drain of color. For a moment, he seemed frozen, as though he was waiting for the words to turn into something else, something less final.

I couldn't look away. I felt like I shouldn't be there, like I was intruding on something too raw, too private, but I was frozen too—caught between wanting to comfort him and knowing I had no words for a grief like this.

DI Rawlins asked Jasper to step outside the room with her for a moment, where another officer would be able to answer his questions in private. She suggested he might want to take a moment.

When Jasper and DI Rawlins left, Hugo was the first to speak. "I imagine he'll have to identify her. Isn't that what they do when someone dies? Awful business. I'll go with him, of course."

Hugo's words jarred me. I couldn't help but think he was taking the death of his mistress remarkably calmly. His initial fluster had faded the moment he began to talk business. And now he was all about practicalities again.

Gillian and Lucas also looked uncomfortable. A murder investigation was hardly an ideal second date.

The picture rose in my mind's eye of everything I had

seen when I walked in on Tamsin's body, right down to the pillow on the floor and the strangely decaying petals.

Sophia left the room and soon a waiter came in with more coffee, bottles of water, and small croissants. Arabella fetched coffee for both Verity and Hugo. The tension was knife-sharp between them. Lucas and Gillian looked more like a devoted couple than they did in that moment.

I was sipping a bottle of cold water when DI Rawlins and Jasper re-entered the room.

Jasper seemed much calmer, though still in obvious shock, and he went to take a seat next to Hugo. Verity stood to hug him. Arabella busied herself pouring Jasper a coffee. He accepted the cup gratefully but his hand shook as he brought it to his lips.

"I'm sorry to have to ask you more questions, Mr. Faringdon," Rawlins said, pulling up a chair next to Jasper. "But at least you'll be more comfortable here. Or would you prefer to be alone?"

Jasper shook his head. "That's the last thing I want. These three are like family to me."

He studiously ignored the rest of us.

"At what time did you leave Willow Waters yesterday?"

"Around three-thirty p.m."

"And what route did you take?"

Jasper looked confused. "I drove home to our house in Chelsea. I took the A40 and the M40."

"How long would you say the journey took you?"

Jasper frowned. "I don't know. Longer than it should have. There were roadworks on the A40 and some bad traffic. I guess it was around two and a half hours or so."

"And had you always intended to return to London on Saturday afternoon?"

"No, I hadn't." He sounded irritable now. "I intended to spend a nice weekend away with my wife, but I had an emergency meeting with a client." He glanced at Hugo. "I'm a hedge fund manager."

"And Saturday evening meetings are common in your business?"

Jasper gave an irritated grunt. "When a large investor wants to meet, we jump if he snaps his fingers."

"And this client snapped?"

"And I jumped."

DI Rawlins's lips set in a firm line. I could tell she wasn't impressed by Jasper's tone, how he'd gone from a man in shock at the death of his wife to one irritated by police questions.

"Would we be able to look at your car, Mr. Faringdon?" she asked. The question was polite enough but I knew it wasn't really a question.

"That seems a little beside the point of all this, doesn't it?" he said, his cheeks reddening.

"It's all standard procedure, I can assure you," Rawlins replied.

"I can't see how," he said sourly, "but fine." He stood and pulled the keys from the inside pocket of his jacket and handed them over to Sergeant Evans, who left the room with them.

"It's the silver Ferrari," he said as Evans was leaving. "A bird excreted on the hood near the driver's side—can you ask them to be careful not to get any in the interior?"

At the mention of bird excrement, I wondered if I might know the bird in question. Normie did love to aim for shiny, fancy cars.

Jasper suddenly got to his feet. His voice rising, he said, "I don't know why I'm being treated like a criminal when the real criminal is out there, roaming free."

DI Rawlins raised her eyebrows. "What do you mean?"

Jasper scoffed. "I'm talking about her stalker."

"Her stalker?" Rawlins repeated slowly.

Jasper shook his head and crossed his arms. "Are you seriously telling me you don't know?" He looked around the room in outrage. "Has no one told the police my wife was being stalked? How did this criminal even get out of jail? That's what I want to know."

"Tamsin Mortimer was being stalked?" Rawlins asked, raising an eyebrow.

"For goodness' sake, all you have to do is a quick Google of her name and it's all there. My wife should have been protected from that monster. Instead she wasted hours and hours speaking to your lot and writing statements and negotiating and waiting until finally he crossed the line and entered our home. Only then did you do something."

Jasper was gathering speed now and I could feel his anger rising and bubbling, the indignation and frustration mingling with his shock and grief.

"My poor wife was terrorized. Absolutely terrorized. She was a strong woman and that creep made her feel vulnerable. On edge. And then it ripped her TV career away from her too. Only in the past few days did she feel like a career was possible for her again." His voice began to crack. "She was just beginning to hope again. And then he was released from prison." He looked around the room wildly. "It must have been him. That stalker murdered my wife and I am going to make damned sure that he pays for his crime."

He paused and took a breath. Suddenly, all the energy went out of him and he deflated like an old balloon. He sat again.

"I'll never forgive myself. She said she'd caught a glimpse of the man, but I made light of it. Ever since he was released from prison, she'd been telling me she'd seen him. I didn't believe her. I thought she was being paranoid."

"We're at the very beginning stages of the investigation, sir," DI Rawlins assured him. Why hadn't any of us mentioned the stalker? I imagined we'd all been focused on our own dealings with Tamsin.

When Sergeant Evans returned, she spoke to him in a low voice and he left again. No doubt he'd been sent to research the stalker. Good.

Verity was trying her best to comfort Jasper, who was mostly ignoring her attempts, preferring to stare out of the window instead. Hugo was on his phone. Arabella looked worried.

A few minutes later, a uniformed officer arrived holding a large piece of paper. Rawlins thanked him, and then turned the paper over. On it was a mug shot.

"That's him," Jasper spat. "That's Malcolm Pritchard."

I went closer. His face was unremarkable and seemed oddly familiar, like a person I might have passed on the street without a second thought. He had short brown hair, dark brown eyes, and a flat nose with wide cheeks. His eyes looked blank, as if he were elsewhere, thinking about something other than the fact that he was being arrested. There was a slight weariness to his expression. Mostly he just looked tired. It was hard to reconcile this image with a man whose passion and obsession had gotten him locked up. I couldn't help but wonder what had driven him to cross that line.

Imogen got up and came to look. Immediately, she turned white. "Oh no," she murmured. "Oh no."

A chill went through me.

"What is it?" DI Rawlins asked.

"I saw him. I met him. I..." she trailed off and turned to me. "Oh, Peony. That *is* who was looking for Tamsin yesterday."

Jasper leapt to his feet. "What? He was *here*?"

Imogen briefly explained that the man in the photo had walked into the room looking for Tamsin. When we'd told Tamsin a man had been looking for her she'd said it was Jasper, looking for her to tell her he had to go to London. But now that she saw his photo, Imogen was able to confirm that the man who'd been in this very room asking after Tamsin was the man who'd spent six months in jail for stalking the British Ballroom contestant.

DI Rawlins immediately turned to Evans. "Get everything we can find out on this man and order a search for him immediately."

Evans nodded grimly and left.

Imogen's eyes began to fill. The poor girl was overwhelmed. I put an arm around her shoulder. "It's okay," I said. "You weren't to know. You passed on the message to me and I told her someone was looking for her. She assured me it was her husband letting her know he had to leave for London. There was no reason to question it."

Jasper was shaking his head. It was a terrible feeling to

know that Tamsin's stalker had been wandering around the hotel and no one had done anything about it. My mind flashed back to Tamsin's body laid out on the bed and I shuddered. I recalled how Imogen told me that Tamsin's stalker had started off by waiting for her outside the studio holding flowers before he began sending them to her home. Now the roses scattered around her corpse made a weird sense, like he was sending her flowers, declaring his twisted love, even after death.

Jasper began pacing. "I need to get out of this room. That man could still be in the hotel. We must find him."

"That's for the police to handle," DI Rawlins said firmly.

"But you didn't even know she'd been stalked!" he shouted. "How can I trust you?"

There was a distraction as Helena came back into the room. "In all this commotion, I forgot my bag with my notebook and my cardigan in it. I just need to fetch it. Sorry to intrude."

As she walked by the photograph, she said, "Oh, that's that nice man who spoke to me yesterday. He complimented me on my bouquet and we had a nice chat about roses. He has trouble with aphids."

Verity began crying again. "We didn't take her seriously," she wailed. "And he followed her here. And now she's dead."

Arabella frowned. "I don't understand it. How could Malcolm Pritchard possibly have found her? Tamsin wouldn't even let herself be photographed in case something ended up on social media. Don't you remember?"

Verity cried even harder. All her makeup had run off her face and she looked younger and more vulnerable than I'd seen her before. "She said she'd seen him outside her house, and we all thought she'd glimpsed a stranger. He must have followed her here. And murdered her!"

And then Helena gasped, clutching her bag to her chest. "It's all my fault," she wailed. "It's my fault that poor girl is dead!"

Chapter Seventeen

"Helena," I said, trying to temper my shock, "what do you mean, it's your fault?"

Helena went to speak then sobbed again.

"Who on earth is this woman?" Jasper demanded.

"What's your fault?" I asked again, trying to calm Helena as best I could so she could explain herself.

"I feel I've as good as killed that poor young woman."

"What is she talking about?" Jasper asked. He began to tug at his hair in frustration.

Helena went white. "I wasn't hiding anything. I just didn't know it would be so important...I...I posted a photo on my Instagram. Yesterday and I tagged Tamsin. Before I knew about Tamsin's stalker."

"What photo?" Arabella asked, her voice icy cold.

"Of the group. It was just a silly post about the weekend flower arranging here at the inn. I was so excited that Tamsin Mortimer was also on the course. I mean, I couldn't believe such a celebrity was doing the same thing at the weekend as me. But when Tamsin said she didn't want any photos of her to be posted, I tried to take it down immediately but I couldn't work it out. I phoned my daughter in the lunch break and she helped me delete it. The post was only up for a couple of hours."

Jasper looked like he'd like to strangle Helena. "And is your profile public?"

She looked completely confused by the question. "I don't know."

"If you've got a public profile, a couple of minutes would have been enough. You might as well have sent my wife's stalker a map of her whereabouts," he said, his voice cold and hard.

She started to cry again. "I didn't know. That's got to be how her stalker found her. And now she's dead."

Helena put her hands over her face and wailed. I guided her to a chair and told her to take deep breaths. It was a silly mistake, and one she had made not knowing how much it could put Tamsin's life at risk. I didn't envy Helena at this moment. A quick snap with her phone and she may well have set in motion a chain of events which culminated in a terrible murder. Jasper looked like he might punch her, and Hugo and Arabella were trying to calm him down.

"Malcolm Pritchard might have come to the hotel, but how did he get into Tamsin's room?" Arabella asked.

Jasper turned to her. "Because the security's rubbish in this hotel. Anyone can come and go."

I thought it was pretty unfair to expect a historic coaching inn in the Cotswolds to have the same security as a London hotel tower, but I kept those reflections to myself. Arabella answered Jasper. "Still, if he knocked on the door, pretending to be hotel staff or something, she'd have looked through the peephole and recognized him. You know Tamsin. She was always looking over her shoulder, especially once she knew that he'd been released from prison."

"She was distracted last night, though," Verity reminded the room. "She was on her phone all night."

"Where is her phone?" Jasper asked, still sounding furious. "That will give us some idea how she spent her last hours. Maybe she took a photograph or something that will help us."

Sergeant Evans sent him a cool look. "Her phone's missing, sir."

Even though I'd been fairly certain that Tamsin's phone was missing, it was still a shock to have the fact confirmed. Had her killer taken it? And if so, why?

Verity seemed almost as upset about the missing phone as she had been about her friend's death. "But that's terrible."

I could picture Tamsin with the phone in its silver case. She'd hardly been parted from it for a second in the short time I'd known her.

"Perhaps we can help," Arabella said. "We were all messaging each other last night."

Immediately, Arabella and Verity pulled out their phones. Arabella had messaged Tamsin to invite her for a drink in the lobby bar, after her room service dinner. Tamsin replied a few minutes later, saying that she was tired and wanted a quiet night in. This was at 8 p.m.

At eleven-ten p.m., Verity had messaged: 'Hope you had a good evening. See you in the morning.' There was no answer. "But I didn't think anything of it. I knew she was probably already asleep. I've always made a habit of texting her goodnight." Her eyes filled again. "It's just something best friends do."

I waited for Hugo to take out his phone, but he didn't move.

Verity gave him a questioning look. "Hugo?"

He shrugged. "Why would Tamsin message me?"

Arabella looked at him sharply, and then I saw the same hard expression enter Verity's eyes. Again, I wondered if *she* knew the truth. Knew that her fiancé had been sleeping with her best friend. But then I recalled how doting Verity was, how in love she seemed as she described the dinner she had alone with Hugo last night. There had been nothing in her voice to suggest she suspected anything. Then again, perhaps she was an excellent actress.

The police did not press Hugo to go through his phone. There was no reason to. He was currently not a suspect— something I was feeling increasingly uncomfortable about.

Next, Jasper pulled out his phone. All his earlier bluster had disappeared. Now he looked completely distraught and I knew that some kind of confession was about to escape his lips. He stared down at the blank screen, reluctant to touch it. Finally, he looked up. In a quiet voice he said, "Our last messages to one another...they were..." He shook his head. "They were harsh."

He stopped and put his head in his hands. Arabella rubbed his back.

Verity looked less forgiving. "What do you mean?" she asked.

"Could you please read out the messages?" Rawlins instructed. "We can go somewhere more private if you prefer."

He shook his head. "I don't want to go anywhere," he said quietly before finally tapping at his phone. "Her last message to me was at nine p.m." He fell silent. I could feel the room holding its collective breath. What was the last thing husband and wife wrote to each other?

He looked up again. "I'm not proud," he said. "She was disappointed in me." He tapped again at his phone.

"*Maybe you can use the time to decide what's more important to you: your work or your wife.*"

Verity grimaced. Jasper kept his head down. Then he said, "She was upset about me rushing back to London when we'd agreed to enjoy this weekend together."

DI Rawlins gave no sign of judgment. She asked, "And that was the last message?"

He turned the phone around so the detective could see the screen. "As you can see."

Rawlins made a note of the message and the time and then asked, "Who was it you were meeting on Saturday night?"

Jasper's irritation flared again. "I cannot see why that is important. It was a work meeting. Instead of wasting time snooping into my business affairs, you should be out looking for the stalker who so obviously killed my wife."

DI Rawlins barely blinked at his outburst. "I can assure you, the search is already underway for Malcolm Pritchard. It's my duty to piece together what happened last night and that involves all the people close to Tamsin Mortimer."

"She's just doing her job," Arabella added. "None of this is her fault. Please be cooperative. It could help things in the long run."

Jasper, now red in the face and sulking like a petulant

teenager, gave DI Rawlins the name of the firm he was meeting with and the name of the CEO. "Gareth Callaghan. We met at his home in Mayfair. I took a taxi there and back so I wouldn't have to worry about parking. It's a nightmare round there. I went straight to bed when I got home. When I woke up this morning, I continued to work. I messaged Hugo and asked him to drive Tamsin home on Monday morning after check-out."

"You didn't message your wife?"

He looked deeply uncomfortable. "As I said, Tamsin was annoyed with me. I thought it would be easier to organize things with Hugo." He looked as though he might cry, then pulled himself together with an effort. "How I wish I'd spoken to Tamsin myself and told her how much I wanted to be with her. How much I loved her."

I felt a lump form in my throat at his raw emotion. It made me want to tell everyone I cared about how very much I loved them.

THE DETECTIVES WERE FINISHED with us for now, but Jasper had the terrible duty of officially identifying his wife's body. Hugo said he'd drive him, which I thought was nice. He said, patting his friend awkwardly, "Then we'll have dinner somewhere quiet." He glanced out the window of the Tudor Rose and added, "Not here. Somewhere away from all of this."

And then Verity began to sob again. "But we can't stay in the suite tonight. I couldn't step foot in there again. Besides, it's a crime scene now. Can't we go home?"

"You can do what you like, but I'm not leaving here until that maniac is caught," Jasper said, with a flash of fury.

Hugo shook his head at her. "We'll stay too, at least until tomorrow. They'll find us another room, love."

Helena, who'd remained white as a sheet and dreadfully quiet through the questioning, picked up her bag and left without a word. The poor woman was riddled with guilt. If only she hadn't snapped that photograph and posted it. A split-second decision might have cost a woman her life.

I wanted to get a moment alone with the detectives to tell them about Tamsin and Hugo's affair. But the detectives were both on their phones and heading out. I wasn't sure how detectives worked, but perhaps they wanted to be there when Jasper identified his wife. Perhaps they'd want to ask him more questions without a roomful of witnesses.

I doubted that Hugo or Arabella would share Tamsin and Hugo's relationship with the police. I didn't want to be the one to tell them, either, if I'm honest, but I couldn't hold back information that might be relevant. Though, with Malcolm Pritchard on the loose, I doubted whether the affair was really connected to Tamsin's murder after all.

Imogen walked over to me, her face still contorted with guilt. "I'm just horrified," she said quietly. "I might have spoken face to face with a murderer yesterday. I should have paid more attention. I feel I'm to blame for that poor woman's death."

I put an arm around her shoulders. "You did nothing wrong. Try to put such thoughts out of your mind." On impulse, I picked up a couple of pink roses, put them together with a bit of greenery and wrapped them with ribbon. Imogen watched me, puzzled, but she didn't hear me whisper, as I let my breath waft over the pink petals:

ROSES PINK, *so soft and bright,*
  Carry sorrow into light.
  Lift the weight from her heart and mind,
  Leave regret and pain behind.
  By petal's blush and gentle stem,
  Let calm and clarity flow to Imogen.
  Let her breathe—of burden free
  So I will, so mote it be

"I JUST WANT TO GO HOME," she said.

I handed her the flowers. As I'd hoped, she leaned in and sniffed at the roses, so I felt sure she'd get the full effect of my healing magic. "Here's my prescription for feeling better. Keep these roses where you can see them and enjoy them." Luckily, Imogen had no idea that roses had circled the dead woman. I wasn't sure I'd be able to look at roses in quite the same way for some time. "Run a bath and get into it with a good book. What happened was terrible but it wasn't anyone's fault except the killer's."

She nodded with a shudder and I was pleased to see she held the roses close to her chest. "I'll pack up and return everything to Bewitching Blooms."

I began to repack the unused flower-arranging gear and supplies when my phone pinged. It was Alex.

"*I didn't go home, Peony, I waited for you on the terrace. I've just seen Arabella and Verity. Where are you? I'm worried.*"

I smiled, suddenly thankful that he was still nearby. I quickly texted that I was fine and tidying up the Damask Room. A few minutes later he was by my side.

Now that we were alone, he took me into his arms and kissed me deeply. Despite everything that had happened, I felt myself melting into the moment. Without the need for words, we both knew that we were there for the other—no matter what.

He helped me clear the room and load the Range Rover. Outside, I was surprised to see that the day was disappearing. The sun was low in the sky, the air cool. We'd been inside the Tudor Rose for hours, embroiled in the burgeoning investigation.

"I'll drop this off at the shop," I said to Alex. "Can you meet me back at my place? I think I'm going to need your help."

"Of course," he said. He kissed me goodbye and got into his Jaguar.

I jumped into the Range Rover, desperate to get on the road. My nerves were jangled and I was kicking myself for not getting to the detectives in time to tell them about Tamsin's affair. As I pulled out of the gravel drive, the tires crunching beneath me, my hands gripped the steering wheel tighter than they needed to. I glanced down to see my knuckles white against the leather. The countryside stretched out before me, but the dull thrum of a circling helicopter suddenly cut through the quiet with its whirring blades. So, the police were already on the hunt for Malcolm Pritchard. It was a relief. But I still couldn't shake the feeling that another darkness was at play. Something bigger than Malcolm Pritchard.

I switched on the radio and turned the dial until the voice of a news anchor cut through the static.

"Breaking news," a man's voice said. "A woman has been found dead in Willow Waters, a small Cotswolds village, under suspicious circumstances. Police are looking for fifty-two-year-old Malcolm Pritchard in connection with the incident. If you see Mr. Pritchard, call 999 and do not attempt to approach the man, who is believed to be in the Willow Waters area."

I swallowed as I imagined that same photo I'd seen earlier appearing on the news and in local and national papers. Tamsin had been a celebrity. Her death would be big news. I kept my eyes on the road, but my thoughts were elsewhere, racing to fill in the gaps, desperate to make sense of Tamsin's death.

The helicopter noise seemed to grow louder. I shook my head, trying to push it away. I was anxious to get back home, to Alex, and talk through everything that had happened in the last few hours.

I felt as though I, too, had let Tamsin Mortimer down. I had sensed trouble around her. Her roses had insisted on wilting when she touched them. Added to Jessie Rae's warnings about roses and danger, I now felt that I'd been incredibly blind. Well, I couldn't bring Tamsin back, but I was determined to help apprehend her killer.

But how? I felt as though I was grasping at shadows. Something I'd seen or heard was trying to get my attention, but what was it?

Chapter Eighteen

W hen I arrived at Bewitching Blooms, the shutters were down and the whole street looked strangely empty. It was as if everyone in the village had decided to stay indoors. It was Sunday, late afternoon.

I unloaded the Range Rover as quickly as I could single-handed, stacking everything just outside the door. Then I pushed up the shutters and entered the silent shop, propping open the door with a heavy bucket of roses. It was already getting dark, so I flicked on the lights. Char had left the shop in pristine condition and I silently thanked my lucky stars for such a good housemate and fellow witch. I unpacked the boxes of materials in a rush, the desire to be at home with the people I loved overwhelming me. I hadn't even had the chance to talk to Alex properly. I ran the buckets of flowers into the shop, carefully placing them in the refrigerated area to stay fresh. I had so much more to return than I had counted on. The day's events meant we hadn't made any of the complicated arrangements and bridal bouquets. As I picked up a bucket, I stopped to smell the white and pink roses Imogen had so carefully chosen and wondered if Verity would postpone her wedding now, and if Arabella would ever get her wish to make her daughter's bouquet with her own hands.

I went back to the car for a last load, then, holding a bucket of roses in hand, I went back into the shop only to find that there was a man standing inside. I was startled and it was all I could to do to stop myself from dropping the bucket with surprise. He was wearing a brown jacket and dark trousers but his face was partially hidden by shadow. Gathering myself, I said, "I'm sorry, we're closed." It was a fact that was patently obvious, what with the shutters halfway down and the shop so empty.

The man stepped forward. I recognized him immediately: short brown hair, dark brown eyes, and a flat nose with wide cheeks. There was a weariness about him and his eyes were tinged with fear.

The bucket slipped from my hand.

It was Malcolm Pritchard.

The crash of the bucket hitting the floor, the slosh of cold water around my feet, pulled me out of my momentary shock.

I couldn't believe that I hadn't noticed I was being followed. I threw my hands into the air and was about to cast a freezing spell when he held up his own hands and in a low, sad voice said, "Please, you must help me. The police are looking for me, but I didn't kill Tamsin Mortimer. I loved her. I would never hurt her."

His eyes were wide open and I could tell the fear he was

feeling was real. But did it come from being hunted by the police or from being innocent?

Okay, so I didn't throw him against the wall with my powers, but I didn't put my hands down either.

"Who are you?" I asked. It seemed like a good idea to play innocent while I figured out what to do. My phone was in my bag, still in the car. I could run out, slam the door and lock this man inside my shop. It would give me enough time to get to my phone and call 999.

"My name is Malcolm Pritchard. I...I saw you through the window. You were teaching the class that Tamsin was taking. She looked so lovely. Roses were the perfect flower for her."

I shuddered, remembering how her body had been haloed in roses.

He continued, "You looked so calm, I felt drawn to you. I think you are the only one who can help me."

He said the words simply. I moved closer. And as I did, I immediately got the sense that he was not a danger to me. I scanned his person for any obvious weapons. Nothing. Then I glanced at the door, still propped open with a bucket of flowers. If I needed to make a quick exit, I was much nearer the door than he was. I didn't relax completely–I'm not stupid–but I dialed my panic down.

Choosing my words carefully, I asked, "How do you know Tamsin Mortimer is dead?"

"I was at the Tudor Rose Inn. I know that I shouldn't have been there, but I just needed to see her face, even from afar." His voice began to choke. "I saw the police. I saw them take away the...take her away." He was nearly in tears now. His grief was sincere, and it was painful to see. I thought about how fans sometimes reacted when a celebrity died. Even if they'd never met the person, they felt an intimate connection. The grief was as real as if that person had been in their own family.

But this didn't mean that Malcolm Pritchard hadn't killed Tamsin. Maybe he'd tried to visit her. He'd been inside the Damask Room asking Imogen about Tamsin. As Jasper had pointed out, the security at the Tudor Rose Inn wasn't top-level. He could easily have got to the suite where she was staying. If he'd found a way to get in, what might have happened?

Perhaps, in fear, she had attacked him first. Had a dangerous mix of anger and adoration overcome him and led to him smothering her with a pillow? His grief could be as real as his guilt.

I swallowed and took a deep breath. The pretty pink and white roses had spilled out when I dropped the bucket and when I looked down I couldn't help but see Tamsin's body again and its macabre arrangement of petals. In a voice as even as I could muster, I asked, "Why do you think I can help you?"

"I told you. I saw you at the inn. The way you were talking to Tamsin, I felt she was safe with you. I think you have a kind face."

I was chilled, knowing that I had been watched without my realizing it. Perhaps simply by being around Tamsin we had all been watched, been assessed and judged. But then his choice of words struck me. "Was she unsafe at other times?"

The irony of asking her stalker this was not lost on me.

Malcolm nodded solemnly. "I knew she was in danger. Those closest to her were not to be trusted. I saw everything."

It suddenly occurred to me that if this man *hadn't* killed Tamsin, then he was probably more informed than the most dedicated private investigator, following Tamsin and seeing who she met with, where she went. And yet I couldn't let go of the very fact that he had gone to jail for persistent stalking. I could still hear the sadness in Jasper's voice as he described Tamsin's plight. The words echoed through me again. *My poor wife was terrorized. Absolutely terrorized. She was a strong woman and that creep made her feel vulnerable. On edge. And then it ripped her TV career away from her too.*

I stared hard at Malcolm. He was the most obvious culprit, the person who had made her feel so unsafe. Who had been sent to jail for his obsession and so had reason to want to punish Tamsin. And yet I could sense that the love he felt for her was real for him—even if it was terribly and horribly misguided. It didn't feel like I was standing in front of a cold-blooded murderer. It felt like I was standing in front of a lost, heartbroken man.

Not knowing what Malcolm Pritchard was capable of made me incredibly uneasy. I stood there, feeling the weight of his gaze pressing into me and for a moment I couldn't shake the tightness in my chest. The uncertainty gnawed at me, a cold, creeping sensation that crawled under my skin and settled in the pit of my stomach. I tried to focus, to find something to ground me. I looked down again at the fallen flowers, their sumptuous petals, the innocence and hope they represented.

Finally, I said, "The police are looking for you. You'll be better off if you turn yourself in. You make yourself look more guilty by running."

But Malcolm shook his head. "No. Then the real killer will get away." There was a passion to his voice and he seemed desperate to tell me something.

I said, "If it wasn't you who killed her, then who did?"

Malcolm came closer and it seemed like he was about to say more when suddenly there was a whirl of motion from behind me. I spun round to see Alex running through the door, looking half-wild. He growled, a deep and intimidating sound, and I realized then that his release from the basement to come find me had been premature—there was still plenty of full-moon werewolf coursing through his system.

Afraid that the animal would take over and he might tear Malcolm to shreds, I blocked Alex's path and put a hand on his arms.

As I did, I felt his wildness, his strength, and his loyalty to me. It all seared through me and I was comforted by each of those qualities, even the wildness. "It's all right," I told Alex. "He didn't hurt me. He's going to turn himself in to the police. He's going there right now, aren't you?"

Malcolm looked petrified. He whispered a *yes* and then rushed past Alex and ran out into the evening.

Alex turned to chase him but I held him back, using the force of my magic to keep hold of him.

"What are you doing?" he asked, still growling. I placed a hand on his chest and felt the thump of his heart, keeping my palm there until it had quietened and the wildness had disappeared from his eyes.

Alex looked pained. "You let him get away. What if he's a killer? He could have hurt you."

He took me into his arms then and I felt safe and warm. I

let my body relax into the embrace and rested my head against his chest.

"I couldn't bear it if anyone hurt you," he said.

"I'm all right," I said into the softness of his shirt. "It's okay. You can't risk exposing yourself by running after that man." I didn't tell Alex that I wasn't certain he could be trusted in his near-wild state, that there was still the possibility that the beast could usurp his rational mind.

I took a moment to breathe. If Malcolm didn't turn himself in, and I suspected he wouldn't, then the police would find him soon enough.

I pulled out of our embrace and said as much to Alex but he looked unconvinced. "I can still catch up to him. I have his scent. I'll deliver him to the police."

I shook my head. "No. You're too close to..." I struggled to find the right words. "Your other self."

His mouth set in a grim line. "Peony, I can restrain myself. I've spent a lifetime doing just that. I would feel a hundred times better if I knew that maniac was going to be locked up again. He followed you here, he tracked you down at your place of work. He could do it again and he could hurt you."

It was so hard to explain why I was defending a convicted stalker but I knew I had to try. "I never felt I was in danger," I said. "He only developed an obsession for Tamsin, you know. No one else. He believed she wasn't safe."

Alex made a sound more like a snort than a growl, which I took as progress. "She wasn't safe from *him*."

"I know I sound a little crazy, but I'm not so sure that's true." I couldn't explain the feeling I had, but it was such a convenient solution. Tamsin's stalker, released from prison, tracked her down and killed her. A man who'd never exhibited violence. I knew it was possible, of course, but I also hoped the police would explore all possible suspects before concluding that Malcolm Pritchard had killed Tamsin and arresting him for her murder.

Alex sighed loudly. "I know that look," he said. "What are you thinking?"

"I can't believe I'm saying this, but I need to talk to my mother. The spirits were giving her warnings about this weekend, but they were so vague. Now that Tamsin is dead and I saw her body, maybe my mother can contact them again and I can ask questions."

Alex shook his head like I was crazy, but hey—this is what he signed up for when he agreed to start dating a witch. And it wasn't like dating a werewolf was a walk in the park either.

He placed his large, strong hands in mine. "So, let's go get Jessie Rae," he said. "I'll even pick her up. After the day you've had, I think you should go straight home." He hesitated, then admitted, "I'll follow you home and make sure no one else is following. Then I'll fetch your mother."

I loved his concern. Alex was going to be by my side no matter what. Even if it involved my mother.

I went to the box of supplies I'd brought back from the Tudor Rose and found a reel of red ribbon that Tamsin had used yesterday to tie together her bouquet. She'd been on edge and turned the reel in her hands over and over, lost in thought.

I said, "Maybe if I take something tangible of Tamsin's, I'll get something tangible back."

I quickly texted my mom and told her I needed to speak with her. Alex would pick her up.

She replied instantly with a thumbs-up emoji.

Say what you want about my eccentric mom, but you had to love that about Jessie Rae: she would show up for you with no questions asked.

Chapter Nineteen

"Since you're here," I said to Alex, "then you can help me bring in the rest of the flowers."

I gave him a smile, trying to lighten the mood. But I could tell Alex was still worried about my safety. I wished there was a way I could show him that I could take care of myself, that I had been doing it for years, but I didn't think it would make a difference. It was in Alex's nature to want to protect me.

Together we brought in the rest of the flowers and then I locked up the shop.

During the short journey, I tried to focus my mind on Malcolm Pritchard. I'd had the strong sense he was not dangerous, at least not to me. And the love he felt for Tamsin, however misguided, emanated from him, as did a certain meekness which kept this man in the shadows, choosing to observe from afar rather than get involved. It was hard to imagine him angry and violent enough to kill Tamsin. But he had violated her privacy and made her feel uncomfortable in her own home. Maybe this had laid the foundations for something more sinister later. But my gut told me no.

By the time I arrived at home, full darkness cloaked the village. Warm lights spilled from the farmhouse and when I saw that familiar brick and stone I felt a slight easing in my chest. It had been a long and awful day but it wasn't over yet.

As I stepped out of the car, the cool evening air filled my lungs, and the smell of fresh earth and pine from the woodland hit me, grounding me in a way nothing else could.

I walked in and was greeted by the comforting smell of wood smoke. I couldn't face talking to anyone just at the moment, so I headed straight upstairs to my bedroom. Blue appeared and ran up the stairs behind me. She meowed insistently and I picked her up. "I missed you today, my darling," I whispered against her fur. I felt that she knew it and was doing her best to comfort me. I also hoped that having my familiar near would help me remember whatever it was that was eluding me.

Blue jumped up on the bed and watched me strip off everything I'd worn today. All of it went into the washing basket. Then I headed into the en-suite and indulged in a long, hot shower.

By the time I came back downstairs, my hair still damp, wearing my comfiest jeans and a blue sweater, I smelled something delicious bubbling on the stove. Jessie Rae was already here.

Alex, Char, and my mom were in the kitchen, sitting at the table with a pot of tea. Loki was curled up on my mom's lap and Norman was perched on Char's shoulder. I was reminded of that moment earlier when I'd wanted to tell everyone I cared about how I felt. I smiled. "Thank you all for being here. You mean the world to me."

"Ah, luvvie," Mom said. "You are my heart, and my pride and joy."

Char looked a bit alarmed at my emotional outburst and Alex turned toward me, telling me everything I needed to know with the expression in his eyes. His hands were still showing the signs of his wild attempt to escape, and so I fetched some of my magic salve and rubbed it carefully on his hands, using my magic to help him heal more quickly. I felt the connection between us as I touched him gently, and it helped calm me.

When I was finished, Jessie Rae said, "I heard on the news that poor young woman from the dance show was murdered. And Alex has filled me in on everything else. What a terrible thing. How are you, my love?"

I so appreciated that Mom thought of me first. I squeezed her hand. "I'm fine."

As I took a seat next to Jessie Rae, relieved I didn't have to find the words to tell the story of Tamsin's death, Blue appeared and jumped into my lap. Char handed me a cup of herbal tea and said, "I'm sorry, Peony."

"Nasty business," Norman agreed.

I nodded. "What's important now is that we get to the bottom of what happened to Tamsin."

"And you need my help, luvvie?" my mom asked. She sounded as surprised as I was that I was actually asking for her help. Normally, I tolerated—rather than enlisted—my mom's communions with the spirit world, but right now I couldn't see any other way of making all these stray ends add up.

I set the reel of red ribbon on the table. "The words of your vision last night stayed with me," I said to my mom. "I dreamed of roses and thorns and blood. And then today I found Tamsin, surrounded by withering rose petals. But I can't make sense of it. Something's telling me that she didn't die at the hands of her stalker, even though all clues point to him."

Alex shot me a hard look. I could see he was still annoyed that I'd let Malcolm go. But he would have to trust me on this one.

"I brought the ribbon Tamsin was handling yesterday. I thought it still might contain some of her essence."

"Good thinking, luvvie," my mom said, picking up the ribbon and turning it over in her hands, just as Tamsin had. "You want me to call on the spirits and ask for their help?"

"Exactly," I said, still not quite believing it. "Maybe they can tell us something about the passage of Tamsin to the other side. Someone sped her on her way before her time."

Jessie Rae nodded and then Char moved around the kitchen, dimming the lights and lighting six candles which she set back down in the center of the table. The flames flickered and danced, casting shadows across our faces.

Jessie Rae sat with closed eyes. I smelled the herbs in my tea and sipped, trying to steady myself. My mom began to move slowly, swaying side to side, her hands gracefully making small, sweeping circles which began at her sides and moved up and out until they were above her head. Her gold bracelets jangled and the sleeves of her rust-colored tunic pooled at her elbows.

I had watched my mom commune with the spirits and reach beyond the veil countless times, but tonight was different. Tonight, we were searching for something lost, something that had been violently torn away from the world.

My mom's swaying intensified and her face tightened in concentration. Her eyes were closed, but her breathing had changed—slow, deep, like she was diving into the depths of the world's mysteries. The room seemed to grow colder, the shadows across the table stretching longer, as if the spirits themselves were drawn in. And then, a sound—a soft, almost imperceptible moan escaped from my mom.

Her eyes suddenly snapped open. Her pupils were dilated. She stared into the distance, beyond us all, beyond the walls, and I knew that the spirits were with her.

"Oh wise spirits," she called out, her voice trembling with intensity, "tell us about our dearly departed Tamsin's journey to you."

She waited, arms outstretched, her fingers twitching slightly, the connection growing stronger.

"Ohhh, ohhhh," she moaned. "There is deception here."

I swallowed.

Then my mom began to speak and I knew the spirits were speaking through her. "Do not believe their lies. Love is not love that alters when it alteration finds."

She drew a deep breath and then continued:

"A rose, though lovely, cannot last;
Its petals fall, its color fades,
Just as life is swiftly passed."

ROSES AGAIN. Roses and lies.

Jessie Rae's trance broke and, exhausted, she sat back down at the table. Char squeezed her shoulder and Alex poured her another cup of tea. It was the first time he had seen my mom commune so directly with the spirits. I was a little amused to see that he looked unimpressed. To my mom, he said, "You had a spirit who quoted poetry, but they could have been more helpful. We don't even know if the killer is male or female. Only that they tell lies, which seems like something we could have worked out for ourselves."

Jessie Rae bristled. "The spirits don't live in our world or operate by our rules. Don't be ungrateful."

"I apologize, Jessie Rae," Alex said. "I just feel so frustrated. I've been away this weekend and when I got back Peony was caught up in a murder investigation." He gave me another pointed look and said, "Can you take me through everything that happened so we can try to make sense of your mother's message?"

I nodded. He had a point. Poor Alex condemned to his dungeon, frantic because of a sense I was in danger. He was involved in this mystery now because of me. The least I could do was fill in the gaps. And now that Char was also here, she could help us, too.

"I think we should start by making a timeline," I said.

"I've got a whiteboard in my bedroom," Char said. "I've been using it to write down spells."

"Oh, what a good lassie," Jessie Rae said. "That's the way to strengthen your magic."

Char returned from the bedroom with a whiteboard completely covered in black marker. With a small smile she swiped her hand and said a quick spell and the words disappeared.

"Impressive," Alex murmured.

Jessie Rae shot him a hard look as if to say, *Hey, I just contacted the spirit world but you're more impressed by a small spell?* To Char she said, "Let's start by writing my message from the spirits at the top."

Char looked amused but obliged.

"Love is not love," I repeated, following the words. "That's Shakespeare. Could it mean someone had a connection to Shakespeare? Someone who studied literature? Or maybe an actor?"

Char frowned. "Love is not love that alters when it alteration finds. Could Tamsin have been killed because something important had changed? But what? Was something different for Tamsin this weekend, Peony?"

I thought hard, trying to organize the timeline of the weekend. Alex could see I was straining to remember everything and in his calm way asked me just to start from the beginning—who first spoke to Tamsin and when.

First, we filled them in on seeing Tamsin and Hugo at lunch on Friday.

Mom looked shocked. "She was having lunch in public with her best friend's fiancé? That shows very poor judgment."

I hadn't even thought of that. If I'd recognized her from TV, how many other people had? And as Arabella had told her when I'd overheard them, someone had recognized the pair of them and word had got back to Arabella. How many people really knew about the affair between Tamsin and Hugo?

"Then what happened?" Char wanted to know. She leaned in as though unable to bear the suspense.

"I saw Tamsin having breakfast on the terrace before the course started yesterday morning. She was with Verity, her best friend, Hugo, Verity's fiancé, and Verity's mother, Arabella. When her husband Jasper arrived I realized then that the man I'd seen her with was actually Verity's fiancé."

"But are you certain they were lovers? Perhaps they were just meeting as friends or planning a surprise for Verity."

"Someone saw them kissing," I informed my mother.

Alex nodded. "And the two people we saw looked like they were having a lover's tiff. He threw down his napkin and stomped away from the table. Very poor form."

"These celebrities and their affairs," Char said, as she continued to note down our observations.

"You'd think they'd be too busy to be sneaking around like teenagers," my mom added.

"And then the course started," I continued, ignoring the commentary. "Everyone introduced themselves. Tamsin asked the group not to post photos of her online because she was trying to avoid the limelight. I already knew that Tamsin had a stalker and that had abruptly ended her chances on British Ballroom, but she told the class briefly about it. It turns out Helena, one of the group, was excited a celebrity was on her course and had already posted a photo to Instagram. She didn't know how to delete it so it was up for hours before her daughter managed to take it down."

"I sometimes think," my mom said to no one in particular, "That it's safer communing with the spirits than the Internet."

Char laughed and told her to stop being so silly. "Not

everyone has a stalker following their every move," she said. Then she chuckled and turned to Norman, "Though sometimes it feels that way..."

He playfully pecked her on the shoulder and then flew off to perch on the kitchen countertop. "I know when I'm not wanted," he said, sulkily.

"Okay, so that's how Malcolm Pritchard found Tamsin at the Tudor Rose," Alex said, ignoring the banter.

"We think so," I replied. "But we don't know exactly when he got there. And after talking with him, I'm not convinced he's the murderer."

"Are there any other possible suspects?" Char asked.

"Well obviously Tamsin and Hugo *were* having an affair. Arabella knew about it and confronted Tamsin in the bathroom at the inn. I overheard them talking."

"Woah," said Char. "So Verity's mom knew that her daughter's fiancé was having an affair with her best friend and didn't tell her? That's messed up."

I agreed. "What's more, she kept it secret even when the detectives were asking for important information about Tamsin. And Hugo, well he was acting shifty through the whole questioning."

"Shifty how?" Alex asked.

"Well, it turns out that one of the other guests at the inn, Grace, woke at midnight and went to her window to look out at the full moon. She told us that she saw a couple kissing outside but she couldn't see the faces." I paused, not wanting to gossip about Gillian, but what came next was important to the case. "It transpires that Gillian and another flower-arranging student, Lucas Chen, had a date that night and were walking in the garden."

"Oh dearie, not another romantic involvement for Gillian Fairfax," my mother muttered. "She doesn't tend to choose well, that woman."

Again, I ignored the commentary and continued. "But then Grace interrupted and said that it definitely wasn't Lucas she saw—the silhouette of his hair was bigger and Lucas has a close crop. And that's when she also mentioned seeing a light go off. Verity blurted out that must have been Hugo, who'd got up in the night to use the bathroom. What she didn't realize is that she was implicating her fiancé, who now doesn't have an alibi for part of that night."

Char's hand was flying across the board, noting down the important details.

"And where was Tamsin's husband all this time?" Alex asked.

"In London. He'd left in the late afternoon to have a business meeting. He runs a hedge fund with Hugo."

"And Tamsin, what did she do on Saturday night?" Alex asked.

"Verity and Hugo had a couple's massage and then dinner, just the two of them in the restaurant. Verity said she invited Tamsin to dinner and she declined. The inn's manager, Sophia, brought Tamsin room service herself and noted that she was messaging someone on her phone, upset."

"Hmmm," Alex said. "Is it possible Tamsin left her room and that was her outside kissing Hugo?"

"It's possible," I agreed.

"But does that make Hugo a suspect?" Char asked. "If he was having a risky affair with her, isn't it also possible he loved her?"

Anything was possible when it came to matters of the

heart. Love, passion—they made people do crazy things. "Maybe. But Alex and I also saw them arguing in the restaurant. It's so hard to know what goes on with two people behind closed doors."

"I wish we knew why they argued. What if he was afraid Tamsin was going to tell Verity?" Alex suggested.

"That would blow up his whole life. His business partner is Jasper. The two couples' lives are completely interweaved."

"Awwwkkkward," Char said, drawing out the word.

After a moment, Alex said, "What about Jasper? Who's to say he was in London the whole time? What if he knew about the affair and was angry enough to kill Tamsin?"

"He seems to have an airtight alibi for most of the night," I said. "But it is possible that he drove back to Willow Waters unnoticed. It's not that far from London and, on quiet roads, he'd make good time." I paused. "And of course there's also the matter of the life insurance."

"Life insurance?" Char asked.

Hugo's words came back to me. *The company pays for the policy. If Jasper died, Tamsin would get five million; if she died, he would get the same amount. Should I die, Verity is my beneficiary and as soon as we're married, she'll be added to the policy.*

"Jasper would receive a cool five million if Tamsin died," I replied.

"Woah," Char said. "I mean, that's a motive there, surely."

Alex looked less convinced. "That's not unheard of in business circles. Jasper likely didn't need the five million. That kind of money is pocket money to hedge fund managers. It certainly wouldn't warrant him killing his wife." I realized that Alex was probably in that category too. While five million would be life-changing for me and nearly everyone I knew, Alex was clearly in a different league financially.

Char nodded, but added the note anyway, "What about Verity's mum? Why did she keep the affair secret? Is something in it for her?"

I shrugged. "It does seem weird that she didn't tell her daughter the truth. I mean, what mother would want her child to marry someone they know is having an affair? In the bathroom, she warned Tamsin not to say anything, but what if she wanted to end the affair herself—permanently?"

"Dark," Char said.

"You've spent time with her, Peony," Alex said. "Do you think she could be capable of something like that?"

"On the surface, no. She's a friendly and successful businesswoman who's worked really hard to get where she is now. But she does have a ruthless streak. She parlayed her husband's title and ancestral home into a fortune with pure grit and ambition and hard work. She's definitely determined. When she sets her mind to do something, it gets done. She also had a keycard to the suite. It's possible she let herself in while Verity and Hugo were downstairs at dinner. No one would have been any the wiser."

We fell into silence, reading through the timeline Char had constructed on the board.

Outside, Normie was circling and as I watched, a telltale missile dropped on where I imagined the gnomes were gathered.

And then I remembered the poop on Jasper's car. That was the thing that had been bothering me.

I called Norman in and he looked as sheepish as a parrot can. Obviously, he thought I was going to tell him off for bothering the gnomes again, but I had a question for him. I tried to keep my voice casual. "Normie, this is kind of weird, but when you flew off in a huff last night, do you remember if you saw a silver Ferrari."

Char spoke up. "A silver Jag? We passed one last night, Peony, on our way home from dropping Jessie Rae off. Don't you remember?"

"No. A silver Ferrari." I was more interested in when Normie had done his number on Jasper's fancy car. "Do you remember if you pooped on that car?" I asked Norman. "Jasper Faringdon could have gone to London but driven back later that night, killed his wife and returned to sleep in his own bed." I felt sick at the thought.

"Silver and shiny? It was this morning," Norman said. "I was enjoying a morning flight. The sun made it sparkle. Excellent target practice." He wasn't confirming he'd hit a Ferrari, but even so, the timing was wrong.

Hmm, that didn't help us. "There's just too much we don't know," I said, starting to worry that we'd never be able to piece this puzzle together.

"What a shame Tamsin's husband went off for that emergency business meeting. How could he have known it would be the last weekend he would have his wife?" Jessie Rae said, shaking her head.

Alex looked thoughtful. "You know, it must have been quite serious to have a hedge fund manager run back to London on a Saturday night to take a meeting."

Alex had a point. Maybe there was more going on with his and Hugo's business than met the eye. Could it have been in some serious trouble?

I gave Alex a speculative look. "Maybe you might like to shop around for a financial firm to look after your finances."

He raised a brow. "Naturally, I am already with a good firm. Are you suggesting you use me as a decoy to get you into a meeting with the same person Jasper met with last night?" I nodded, pleased Alex had figured out my plan so quickly. "Hugo gave us his name. I doubt he meets with many individual investors, but I bet he'd meet with Lord Fitzlupin."

With a resigned look Lord Fitzlupin said, "So let's go to London."

Chapter Twenty

We set off early Monday morning, Alex behind the wheel of his dark green Jaguar. He was dressed in a very smart charcoal gray suit which brought out the silver tones of his pale blue eyes. Without Hilary asking too many questions, I'd managed to borrow a black pantsuit from her and paired it with a silk shirt I'd bought years ago. Using Alex's impressive name and reputation–Lord Fitzlupin, don't you know–we'd managed to secure a meeting with Gareth Callaghan, the CEO of the firm Jasper had dashed off to London to meet. We scrubbed up pretty nicely, if I say so myself, but how I wished it was under different circumstances.

The manhunt was still going on so I knew Malcolm Pritchard hadn't yet been apprehended. Imogen had opened Bewitching Blooms, saying she felt much better after a good night's sleep. Still, I sent Char in to help her, it was her day off from the coffee shop. If Malcolm Pritchard had any idea of coming into my shop today, Char was well able to take care of him.

I spent most of the journey gazing out at the never-ending highway which stretched out in front of us. The sun had all but disappeared and in its place the sky was white with clouds. I barely noticed the lush green fields of the country-side passing by; my mind was consumed with thoughts of Tamsin and the circle around her. Malcolm Pritchard had warned me that those closest to her were not to be trusted. It was hard to take a convicted stalker seriously, but I sensed that there was some truth to his words, and once I'd paired them with my mom's message from the spirits about lies, I was convinced that there was something, or someone, in Tamsin's life who was not what they seemed.

By the time we pulled up outside the firm's fancy office in Knightsbridge, my stomach was in knots. I felt like so much was riding on this meeting and I was seriously out of my depth in this kind of setting. My life was flowers and good magic, not the fast-paced world of million-dollar deals.

Sensing my unease, Alex took my hand as we traveled up the glass elevator to Callaghan's office on the top floor. He gave it a little squeeze and I smiled. It was silly to be intimidated by a flashy building. And if I was going to be dating Alex, I would have to get used to being around CEOs and high-flying executives. It was part of his world as an English lord *and* a wine importer.

But nothing prepared me for the way Gareth Callaghan greeted Alex. As soon as his secretary led us into his office, Gareth beamed and leapt up to shake Alex's hand profusely. "What a pleasure indeed to meet you, Lord Fitzlupin."

"Alexander will do nicely," Alex said, taking back his hand, which was still being vigorously shaken. "And this is Ms. Peony Bellefleur," he said. "My partner."

I blinked. I wasn't sure if Alex meant partner like girl-friend or if he was making us out to be business partners. In any case, I shook the man's hand.

"A pleasure to meet you, Ms. Bellefleur. And may I say, what a beautiful name. Quite unlike anything I've heard before."

I thanked him and allowed him to pull out one of the two chairs facing his huge teak desk. The view behind him framed the city like a painting. Below, the streets buzzed with a mix of luxury cars, tourists, and shoppers, all heading toward Harrods, just a few blocks away. The greenery of Hyde Park spread out in the distance, its trees a calming contrast to the urban landscape.

As Gareth began his charm offensive to Alex, I tuned out. It was clear he knew Alex's reputation; between his fawning and elaborate sales pitch to showcase how good their firm was, frankly, I grew quite bored. I looked at the photos on his desk: blonde, glamorous wife, two kids, standing in front of a beautiful country cottage. I got the sense that although he worked in a cutthroat business, Gareth was a family man of integrity. He would tell us the truth. While Alex answered some questions about his requirements, I waited for the moment when he'd carry out our plan.

After a grueling ten minutes of finance talk, Alex finally went for it. "I recently met with Jasper Faringdon and Hugo Robinson. They were quite impressive. Do you think theirs would be an appropriate fund for some of my capital?"

I watched Gareth's face intently. There was an awkward pause before he spoke and I could see he was trying to find a diplomatic response. "We could certainly look at adding some extra risk, but I always counsel our clients to be careful of chasing big gains at the expense of the capital."

Alex cocked a brow. It was interesting to see this side of him. For sure I knew he was a businessman, but Alex was obviously a guy who understood how investments work. He said, "Do you believe the hedge fund is too aggressive?"

Again, there was a pause before Gareth answered. With an admirably neutral expression he said, "We are currently in the process of severing our relationship with GoldenBridge."

"Ah, I see," Alex replied, not batting an eyelid. "So one to avoid."

Gareth nodded slowly. "For now, I would say yes. Jasper Faringdon made some big bets that didn't pay off. He is not exactly risk-averse. We prefer firms that are more stable." He let the sentence trail off. Clearly he believed there was no need to say more.

But Alex was here for unequivocal answers. "So, in your opinion the fund may fail."

Gareth gave a small nod of his head. It was enough. We had the answer we'd come for. Jasper and Hugo were in hot water. I thought back to the boastful way Hugo had talked about the fund. Clearly they weren't as successful as they were pretending. Or was Jasper hiding something from his business partner and so-called best friend? If Jasper was in financial trouble, then the sudden death of his wife would prove mighty useful. She was worth five million pounds in life insurance after all.

I tuned out the rest of the conversation, eager to leave and discuss what we'd learned with Alex.

By the time we'd left the building and came out onto the bustling street, my mind was working overtime.

"You were amazing in there," I said. "So knowledgeable and businesslike. And you managed to get Gareth to spill the beans about GoldenBridge so subtly."

Alex grinned. "I admit, I was having a bit of fun." He opened the passenger door of his Jag and I slipped into my seat and buckled up. "Gareth Callaghan was impressive," he continued when he'd settled into his own side of the car. "I might do some business with them. Which stops me feeling bad about meeting under false pretenses."

I nodded. "So...are you thinking what I'm thinking?"

Alex turned to look at me, suddenly serious. "Yes. This adds a new aspect to the case. Now we know that Jasper Faringdon wasn't as successful as we thought, he now has *two* possible motives for his wife's murder. If he didn't know about her affair, his impending financial ruin was motive enough. It seems I was wrong. That life insurance payout may have been more important to him than I'd realized. He could have needed money desperately."

Alex started the engine and the car roared to life. I stared out at the streams of dark-suited men and women as they spilled from buildings and went about their busy mornings. "Terrible, isn't it," I said, "that money could come between husband and wife in such a fatal way."

"Still," Alex said, looking pensive, "there are some other suspects we can't ignore. Hugo. Arabella. And I know what you sense about Malcolm but we shouldn't rule him out."

I nodded grimly. "If only we knew more about how Tamsin died," I said.

Alex looked thoughtful. "You know, I have a friend on the force. I'll put a call in when we stop."

"Good idea."

But I wanted to know more about Tamsin's life as well as her death. Specifically, her home life with Jasper.

And then I had an idea. I said, "Do you think we could make a quick stop before we head back? Jasper and Tamsin's house is in Chelsea—not too far from here. I feel that if we got closer to where she lived, I might be able to use my powers to intuit more about what went on behind closed doors."

Alex was game, so I texted Imogen for Tamsin's address, which was on the booking form for the flower-arranging course. She messaged back straightaway and we headed off.

The traffic was heavy and I tried to calm my frustration. I couldn't help but feel that every minute spent not building our case was time when a murderer was roaming free. I was still certain that Malcolm Pritchard was not our man, but I didn't yet have enough to narrow down the other suspects.

"Here we are," Alex said, turning into a quiet, tree-lined avenue. I was taken aback. "Are you sure this is it?" I asked.

He nodded.

Tamsin's home was more impressive than I'd imagined— an enormous gleaming white townhouse, four storeys high. Entry was via a gated front garden with neat rows of pretty topiary, and white stone steps ascended to a covered porch. The front door looked to be bespoke: a heavy fortress-like affair with a high golden mailbox. Outside was a blue BMW that must have been Tamsin's car. Sadness overcame me then as I realized she would never again pull into her driveway, never again walk into her multimillion-pound home. All her dreams of a new TV career died with her.

The car looked new, too. Shiny but for a scratch on the front driver's side.

Alex cut the engine and used his Bluetooth to phone his friend on the force. I exited the car and stood far enough away from the house that I wouldn't look suspicious, and close enough to tune into its emotional frequencies. Closing my eyes for a moment, I tried to imagine Tamsin and Jasper's life inside that enormous building. I could see a kitchen, Tamsin making smoothies. I saw her eating fruit and yogurt, flicking through a sports magazine. But Jasper wasn't in the picture. I tried to mentally walk around the building, looking inside each tastefully decorated and tidy room. But no, he was nowhere to be found. I opened my eyes again. Either Jasper was away a lot on business, or my intuition was telling me that he was absent in more ways than just the physical. I was suddenly certain that Tamsin had felt alone in her marriage. Which tied in with the fact that she'd had an affair.

I got back into the car, drained of energy. Alex, too, looked paler than when I'd left him. "What is it?" I asked.

"You were right about the pillow," he said. "The police believe she was suffocated by a pillow over her face, time of death about two a.m. Certainly, in the early hours of the night."

I shuddered. Even though I'd believed this was how she'd died, it still felt horrible to have it confirmed. What a scary, sad way to die.

We were silent for a moment, our thoughts with Tamsin, and then Alex started the car and we began the drive back from London.

Alex said, "Did you get anything from the house?"

"Yes and no. I couldn't sense Jasper at all. All I could feel was Tamsin's isolation."

Alex took a deep breath. "You know, I only met the man for a minute, but it's hard to imagine him killing his wife."

I nodded. "But if money really was the drive behind her murder, how convenient to be able to blame her death on a stalker who was just released from prison."

"That's true," Alex said, "but we're forgetting Hugo was the other half of the failing GoldenBridge hedge fund. If Tamsin was trying to break up his relationship with Verity to marry him herself, then Hugo had plenty of motive."

"So both Hugo and Jasper could have benefitted from her death."

"How awful," Alex said quietly.

"I wish there was a way we could find out if Jasper knew about the affair."

Alex glanced at me and then said, "I could understand how a man could lose his mind if he thought he was losing the woman he loved."

Maybe Alex had a point. A crime of passion rather than fear of financial ruin. The spirits had certainly indicated love gone wrong. How could we find out?

❧

BEFORE LONG, we were back in the Cotswolds, making our way through the familiar winding lanes. I wound down the window to take deep lungfuls of the fresh, grassy air. Even just a short time in the big city made me grateful for where I lived. I just loved the wide open space, the sense of peace which came over me as soon as I was back in the countryside. Of course, London's big buildings were exciting and so was the bustle, but I would take a rolling hill any day of the week.

The traffic slowed as we approached road construction. Roadworks, they called it here. Sitting atop one of the lampposts and surveying the roadway was a brightly feathered parrot. Of course Norman was back here, seizing the opportunity to poop on the parade of cars which slowed beneath his perch. I watched with fascination and a little horror as he picked and chose which car he pooped on, opting for the shiniest, most obviously new cars.

As our car drew closer, Normie spotted us and, with a wild squawk and mad flapping of his wings, flew away. He knew better than to mess with us.

And then I remembered that yesterday he'd chosen Jasper's car. We were making the exact same journey that Jasper had taken before he knew his wife was dead.

Or before he knew he was about to encounter the police and had to put together a plausible story.

Chapter Twenty-One

Alex dropped me at Bewitching Blooms and with a melting kiss told me he was going to work in Roberto's Coffee Shop so he could be close by if anything were to happen to me. What he meant was if Malcolm Pritchard decided to pay another visit, or any of the other suspects we'd narrowed down in the last twenty-four hours. I thought he was overreacting but when I saw the buckets of the weekend's unused roses waiting to be sold, a chill went through me and I was glad to know he was nearby.

In the back of the shop, I slipped out of my smart dark suit and into jeans and a white shirt and set about opening the store.

It wasn't long before I had my first customer. And then another. And in that way, I passed the rest of the afternoon in a daze, trying to get my head around all Alex and I had discovered in London. I was so frustrated by the gaps in what we knew, how it left me going round in circles. So, I was pleased when a friendly face appeared at the door.

Gillian Fairfax came into the shop looking more frazzled

than her usual sleek self. Her cheeks were flushed, her hair escaping its chignon and there was a look in her eye which I couldn't quite place. Excited but anxious. Curious but nervous. The weekend's events must have brought back terrible memories for her. But I sensed it was more than that. I also didn't think she was here for flowers.

I greeted her warmly and asked if she'd like something to drink. "I was just about to put the kettle on," I said.

She thanked me and took a seat on the stool by the work-top. I made some calming herbal tea and handed a mug to Gillian. She blew across its steaming surface, looking pensive.

"How are you feeling?" I asked.

"A little rattled, Peony, if I'm being honest. Your course was such a tonic for me and then for it to end so horribly..." She trailed off and I gave her hand a small squeeze. I waited, knowing there was more.

She took another sip of tea. "Can I be honest with you?" she asked finally.

"Of course."

"It's Lucas."

Of course it was Lucas.

"He's showing real interest. And well, he's charming, clever, and he's kind. So kind. But I've had such bad luck with men in the past, I told myself I'd never be so foolish again. And yet—I feel there is something different here."

"I agree," I said. And then quickly added in case she thought I was agreeing about her being foolish, "About there being something different about him. I get a good vibe from him. And the way he looks at you, well, there's no mistaking it: it's like everyone else in the room melts away for him."

Gillian blushed like a teenager.

"I think you should trust your heart. You might have made some bad choices in the past but that doesn't mean you can't learn and grow."

Gillian laughed a little bitterly. "*Bad choices* is putting it nicely. I've chosen men for all the wrong reasons. They could advance my career, were fabulously wealthy, or they were young and hot. I'm tired of all that now. But then comes along an absolutely gorgeous younger man who's not shy of a penny or two." She sighed.

"But this gorgeous younger man is a good man. That's the important difference. He can't help his age. Or being rich. And he definitely can't help being handsome! Don't hold that against him."

Gillian laughed. "It's good advice. I must admit, I am really quite smitten."

"Enjoy it," I said. "And don't worry all the fun of a new romance away."

She smiled and thanked me and we chatted for a while about business. I sensed she didn't want to talk about the murder case, so I kept it light. To be honest, it was also nice for me to momentarily push it out of my mind. I'd been consumed by the case from the moment I had come across Tamsin's body. It was nice, even if just for ten minutes, to feel like life was continuing as normal.

Not long after Gillian left, the phone rang. I knew who it was before I even touched the phone.

"Good afternoon, Bewitching Blooms," I said, adopting my professional voice. "How can I help you?"

"Peony," a deep, warm voice said, "it's Lucas Chen."

I smiled. I had a feeling I knew exactly what Lucas was about to say next.

"How lovely to hear from you," I said. "I trust you were able to stay another night at the Tudor Rose Inn?"

"Yes, thank you. They're very kind there. Especially given the circumstances. But, I think I might have left my heart in Willow Waters."

I was so pleased for them both. "Let me guess: Gillian Fairfax."

He laughed softly. "I'm afraid I was indiscreet yesterday. I wish I hadn't been forced to be so ungentlemanly by telling everyone we had kissed in the garden."

"You had no choice," I said. "I'm sure Gillian understands." Of course, I couldn't mention that she'd just been here, discussing him, and hadn't even brought up the fact. "It was the right thing to do."

He sighed. "Thank you. It's been playing on my mind. Which is why I was calling. I'd like to send Gillian some flowers, but I'm not sure what to include. In the garden, she commented on some pretty white asters, but beyond that I haven't a clue. I'd like to really wow her."

I grinned down the phone. I had an idea. "Of course, I can help you with Gillian's favorite flowers," I said. "She's a great lover of soft pastels. But since you're just around the corner, why don't you come in to the shop and make the bouquet yourself? You showed quite the aptitude for arranging on the course and I owe you another bouquet. I think there's nothing Gillian would like so much as a handmade bouquet."

Lucas chuckled delightedly. "What a wonderful idea, Peony. You're quite the Cupid."

I smiled. "All part of the service."

Fifteen minutes later, Lucas was at the store. He looked as excited as Gillian, dressed casually but carefully in an expensive white shirt and dark blue denim. He really was very handsome.

"So," I began, "you mentioned some asters?"

There was a pause. "I'd like to include those if it's possible," he said. "To remember that evening by." A whimsical look came into his eyes. "It was so perfect. Dinner was delicious, and on the drive back to the Tudor Rose we didn't stop talking. Without discussing it, we found ourselves strolling through the gardens. The air was cool, the stars so bright, and the scent of roses from the garden wrapped around us like a soft, fragrant cloak. Every now and then, Gillian would point out a flower or a tree, telling me its name in that confident way she has. I was hanging on every word, not because I cared particularly about the flowers but because she said it. We walked in silence for a while too, the kind of silence that felt comfortable, not awkward. It was only broken by the sound of a frog plopping into the pond nearby. When the moonlight caught her hair, turning it into something almost ethereal, I couldn't help but kiss her."

I looked at Lucas. What a beautiful description of a first date. It was a pleasure to help him impress Gillian. And, without knowing it, he had just helped me with something *very* important.

Together we chose some pale pink roses, some soft sprigs of locally grown lavender, sweet peas in shades of pink and lavender and those puffy white asters. I suggested some sage leaves for greenery. Their subtle, silvery tone complimented the pastels and wouldn't overpower the bouquet. I guided Lucas as he arranged them in a relaxed, loose style, allowing the blooms to gently curve out and create a natural, unstructured look. He finished the arrangement with a silken blush ribbon.

"Gorgeous," I said, standing back to appraise the final bouquet.

Lucas grinned, his white teeth gleaming.

"Why don't you take Gillian to the Tudor Rose Inn for dinner tonight? You can give her the bouquet then."

"Another wonderful idea, Peony. What would I do without you?"

Lucas thanked me for everything and headed out, one happy customer.

And he had given me something invaluable in return.

Thankfully it was closing time. I shut up the shop in a hurry and then drove home as quickly as I could.

"Char," I called out as I stepped in the door. "Where are you?"

"Bedroom," she replied.

Char's door was open and I could see that she was practicing spells with Norman. I smiled. That girl was truly dedicated. She had brought the whiteboard back into her room, its once-white surface now covered in our timeline and list of suspects. I pointed at it and said, "I'm pretty sure I know where Tamsin's phone is."

Char raised a brow. "What? So, what are we waiting for? Let's go get it."

I grinned. I just loved how she was down for anything. Even if that meant taking a leap into the unknown.

Along with Normie, we jumped into Frodo, the old truck, and I told Char to drive to the Tudor Rose. She drove thoughtfully and speedily, humming along to a guitar track I didn't recognize on the radio.

We pulled into the inn and I told Normie to be our watch guard.

"Don't do anything stupid," Char said over her shoulder before turning to me and asking, "So, are you ready to tell me where we're headed?"

"The pond," I said. Now that we were here, I was certain that my hunch was right. I could feel myself being drawn to water.

I led the way, winding along the stone paths and pretty flowerbeds. The pond was tucked away at the far edge of the garden, almost like it was a secret. The water was so still it mirrored the sky perfectly and the edges were softened by overhanging willow trees. Around the pond, the ground was dotted with wildflowers. A small stone bench sat beside the water, half-hidden by a bush of hydrangea in bloom, their petals unfurling like delicate tissue paper.

Char looked at me quizzically.

"It's in there," I said, pointing at the water. "I'm sure of it."

Char let out a low whistle. "Jeez, Peony. Why didn't you tell me to bring a wetsuit?"

I chuckled. "Witches don't need wetsuits," I said.

"A rising spell?"

"You got it. Can you remember one?"

Char nodded, her mouth set in determination. She closed her eyes, took a few breaths and then said:

"From the depths, from the darkened deep,
Where secrets lie, and shadows sleep,
I call on water, earth, and sky,
To raise what's hidden, let it rise high.

. . .

By moonlit beam and gentle tide,
I seek the truth that waits inside.
With willow's touch and crystal bright,
Let the depths release their might.

Oh sacred pond, in you I trust,
Raise what's lost, from water's crust.
From darkened depth to surface bright,
Bring forth what waits in stillness' light.
So I will, So mote it be.

AS SHE SPOKE, the surface of the water began to ripple, first gently, then with more insistence. Something was stirring. It was as if the pond itself had drawn a breath and then slowly, silently exhaled, the water parting.

"Yes," I whispered.

Something was nearing the surface. The pond began to bubble, the water swirling. And then, as the last of the water parted, the object broke through the surface. I recognized the silver phone case immediately. It was Tamsin's cell phone. Char had done it!

"Now," I whispered to Char, "bring it towards you."

Char's eyes narrowed and she held out her hands, straightening her fingertips as if they could reach the phone. In a clear, strong voice she said:

. . .

"Water's flow, pull it near,
Bring it close, without fear.
Let it come, by earth, by sea,
Drawn to me, so mote it be."

FOR A MOMENT, it hovered there—just out of reach—before sinking slowly again. But we'd both seen the silver case. I was certain it was Tamsin's phone. "Leave it. We must let the police retrieve it."

"How did you even know it was here?" she asked.

"Lucas Chen told me he heard the sound of a frog plopping into the water the night Gillian was murdered. But this pond isn't deep enough to spawn frogs. I've never heard frogs croaking here, either.

I had a hunch it was the sound of Tamsin's phone being thrown into the water. Someone didn't want her messages to be discovered."

"It's bound to be ruined," Char said. She looked distressed.

"It's been underwater for two days," I said. "I don't think even our combined magic could revive it. But don't worry. I've got an idea."

Chapter Twenty-Two

I sent Char to check on Normie (that parrot can get himself into mischief if left to his own devices too long) and then headed inside the inn to see Sophia. I found her behind the reception desk. She looked busy, so I quickly asked if Verity, Arabella, Jasper, and Hugo were due to have dinner there that night. She looked a little confused but said yes, they were. "And has Lucas Chen booked a table for two?"

"He has," Sophia said, a slight frown worrying her brow. "Is everything okay?"

"It's perfect," I replied. "Thank you. I'll tell you more soon."

I left and went back to the truck where Char and Normie were waiting.

"Can you drop me at the police station?" I asked. "It's time that the detectives know about Tamsin and Hugo's affair."

Char nodded and soon we were heading back towards the village.

As we drew closer, I began to feel nervous about revealing the affair, but I had already procrastinated long enough.

We pulled up outside the station and Char said she'd wait for me outside.

I climbed the steps with trepidation, knowing that I was soon going to have to stand my ground. Inside, the police station was buzzing with officers. Clearly, they'd deployed more people to work on Tamsin's case. I walked up to the desk, my sneakers squeaking a little on the tile floor. The fluorescent lights buzzed overhead, casting a cold, sterile glow over everything. My palms were sweating, and I wiped them on my jeans before reaching the desk. The officer behind the glass looked up as I approached him. "Can I help you?" he asked.

I took a deep breath, feeling the weight of the moment pressing down on me but I was determined to do the right thing. "I need to speak with DI Rawlins," I said, trying to keep my voice steady. "It's important. I have information about the Tamsin Mortimer case."

The officer's eyes flickered with a mix of curiosity and suspicion and then he picked up the phone. Moments later, the officer hung up and gave a quick nod. "Detective Rawlins will be with you shortly. Take a seat."

I nodded and took a seat on the blue plastic chair opposite. A couple of minutes later, DI Rawlins appeared. She was in her usual crisp suit but there were deep bags beneath her sharp eyes. This case had been keeping her up at night.

"Ms. Bellefleur," she said. "How can I help you?"

I took a breath and said I had important information. She nodded and led me through a security door and to a small room with a table and chairs. An interview room. I then told her everything I knew about the affair between Hugo and

Tamsin. She didn't look shocked. But she didn't look happy, either. "And you're only telling me this now?"

I started to make excuses and stopped myself. She was right. I should have given her this valuable information sooner. However, I had no sense of surprise from the detective. "Did you know about the affair?" I asked, hoping this was old news.

DI Rawlins shook her head. "No, but in this line of work you see the dark side of humanity. An affair which would rupture a friendship group is not as uncommon as you might think."

"But this casts a new light on the case, doesn't it? Now Arabella Ainsworth has motive to kill Tamsin to end the affair which would ruin her daughter's opportunities. Jasper has motive to murder his cheating wife. Hugo has motive to protect his relationship with Verity if Tamsin was pressuring him to come clean. I witnessed their heated argument on Friday, after all. Maybe that's what it was about."

DI Rawlins let out her breath. "Perhaps. But to be honest with you, Ms. Bellefleur, we feel we already have our culprit."

I sighed. "Malcolm Pritchard?"

"Yes," DI Rawlins said simply. I was losing her interest. I tried to fight the well of frustration bubbling up. "I have other information which might make you question that," I said.

Rawlins raised one eyebrow. Clearly she was beginning to believe that I was wasting her time. I told her that the investment firm Jasper had a last-minute meeting with on Saturday night was severing ties with GoldenBridge hedge fund.

Rawlins nodded. "Yes, we already know. It's unfortunate timing for Jasper Faringdon, but there are many aggressive investment advisors out there. I read about them all the time in the papers. They may be big risk-takers but they rarely kill their wives."

I stared at DI Rawlins. I couldn't believe that her mind was so set on Pritchard as the murderer that she couldn't see what was right in front of her eyes.

"I think I know where Tamsin's phone is."

She definitely looked more interested now. "Where?"

I told her about the pond and my theory about frogs, not that I'd definitely spotted it, though I may have let her think I'd glimpsed a flash of silver. She seemed very pleased. "This will likely show evidence of messages from Pritchard. Phone calls. Why else would he take pains to get rid of it?"

Swallowing my frustration, I took a breath. "I know you feel like all energies need to be on finding Malcolm Pritchard but I think there's one more thing you really should look at. Take a look at Tamsin Mortimer's car."

Rawlins looked confused.

"Please, trust me on this one."

DI Rawlins merely looked at me and finally said, "You're very good friends with Alex Stanford, I understand. Lord Fitzlupin."

"Yes." I wondered why she cared or what that had to do with anything.

"And his lordship is good friends with my superior. So, yes, Ms. Bellefleur. We'll follow up on your leads. But please don't waste my valuable time."

Ouch. It was pretty clear that DI Rawlins did not relish being forced to follow up on my suggestions because Alex was friends with someone higher up in the CID.

However, since she was pretty much telling me she'd let me be part of the investigation, I went on. "And there's one more thing," I said. "Can you spare a few moments of your time and come to the Tudor Rose this evening? Seven-thirty p.m.?" To seal the request I promised her that Alex would be there too.

DI Rawlins was beginning to look exasperated but she agreed to my request—even if it was just to get me out of there so she could go back to work.

I left the station, now certain that I knew the identity of the killer.

But could I prove it?

I asked Char to drive us back to the farmhouse. She switched on the radio. The news was underway.

"Breaking news," the reporter announced. "The hunt for Malcolm Pritchard has ended. Police apprehended Pritchard at a motorway gas station near London. Mr. Pritchard was wanted by police in connection with the murder of tennis champion and British Ballroom celebrity Tamsin Mortimer."

I shook my head. So, Malcolm had been caught. If only he had turned himself in to the police as I'd suggested. I had a bad feeling that the wrong man was about to be punished for murder. I had to find a way to stop it.

Back at the farmhouse, I asked Char to bring her whiteboard back to the kitchen.

"Who had access to Tamsin's room?" Char asked, studying the whiteboard.

"Arabella, Verity, Hugo, Jasper," I said.

"And the hotel staff," she added.

I remembered the chambermaid who'd come to Tamsin's room just after I found her.

"I know that look," Char said. "You're plotting something."

I grinned. "Could you call the Tudor Rose and book a table for four people for this evening? Say it's for Peony and apologize for the late notice. I'm going to text Jessie Rae and Alex and ask them to meet us there."

Char nodded and I left her to freshen up. In the bathroom, I splashed some cool water on my face and stared into the mirror. If I was going to pull off my plan, I would need nerves of steel tonight. I only hoped I was up to the task.

I called Alex and told him about our 'date' tonight. "And can you stop at a phone store?" I told him what I needed.

AT 7:15 the four of us entered the Tudor Rose's beautiful dining room. Char had changed into a pink velvet dress with a black leather biker jacket; my mom was wearing a silver tunic with matching wide-legged trousers, while I had changed into a simple black shift dress with a small black handbag. Alex wore a dark suit. As a foursome, I suppose we made quite an impression as the maître d' showed us to our table. It was quieter than normal. I figured not many people wanted to dine where someone had recently been murdered upstairs.

Verity, Jasper, Hugo, and Arabella were on the next table over. Gillian and Lucas were also here. As were Roberto and Frederick. I'd spoken to Roberto myself and asked him to bring his partner here tonight. I wanted them to hear this.

Gillian seemed happier than I'd seen her in a long time. When I greeted her and Lucas, she told me how much she'd liked the arrangement he'd made her. She took his hand as she spoke and said, "I think you've got a star pupil in your class." It was nice to think someone had learned something, in spite of the tragedy.

We settled at our table. At 7:25 I got a message from DI Rawlins. It simply said they were nearby. I glanced around the dining room. I suspected at least one of the diners was an undercover cop. At least, I hoped so.

My stomach was in knots but it was time to enact my plan. I nodded at Alex who gave me a smile of encouragement.

I approached Verity's table and asked how everyone was holding up.

Arabella answered first. "We're very sad, of course. Still processing what's happened, really. But there is some solace in knowing that the police have apprehended Malcolm Pritchard."

I looked at each of their faces. Verity looked like she had been crying all day, her eyes and skin puffy; Hugo looked like he wanted to be anywhere but at that table. And Jasper, well he just looked blank. It was hard to get a read on what he was feeling. He reached for the bottle of red wine at the center of the table and topped up his empty glass.

I took a breath and then said, in a clear, commanding voice, "But Malcolm Pritchard didn't kill your wife, did he, Jasper?"

Jasper set down the bottle. He stared at me, clearly taken aback. "I beg your pardon?"

I opened up my handbag and took out 'Tamsin's' phone. I'd had Alex buy a silver phone case and I'd slipped an old phone into it. If you didn't look too closely, it could pass for Tamsin's phone. Calmly, I laid the silver case on the table in front of Jasper.

He went pale.

"It's Tamsin's," I continued. "I found some very interesting messages on this phone." I held his gaze, hoping the bluff would work its own magic.

"You couldn't have," Hugo shouted, jumping up from his seat to grab it, but I got there first. "The phone was underwater!" he shouted. "Everyone knows that ruins it."

The other three people at the table turned to stare at Hugo.

Slowly, Arabella said, "Hugo, how did you know where her phone was?"

Hugo, realizing what he'd done, began to gasp for air. "I... It was a guess. I guessed."

Verity began to shake. "Oh, no," she cried. Her eyes widened as she began to piece it all together. "It *was* you in the garden kissing Tamsin, wasn't it? I tried not to believe it, to block it out. She was my best friend, and you're my fiancé, but I saw the way you two looked at each other." She shook her head in disbelief. "I've been such a fool."

Arabella looked appalled. Her family's secrets were all spilling out now, and very much in public.

Hugo, too, was aghast. "No. It wasn't like that. I love you, Verity. You have to believe me."

I looked at Hugo and tightened my grip on 'Tamsin's' phone. I was guessing all over the place, but so far, my guesses were turning out to be true. "Tamsin's text messages to you threatened to tell Verity everything if you didn't leave her and marry Tamsin instead."

All Hugo's careful poise had disappeared. He was pale and shaking, imagining his whole world being swept out from under his feet. He turned to his fiancée. "I never would have left you. I'm sorry, Verity. It's you I love. It always has been. That's why I wanted to delete the text messages on Tamsin's phone. But I couldn't work out how to get into it. So I threw it in the pond instead."

I turned to Jasper, who had been taking this all in with silent horror. He looked at each of the three faces before him. "Monsters," he said. "You *all* knew. I can see it now."

Verity jumped up and screamed at Hugo. "You killed Tamsin! Don't touch me!"

"No," Hugo cried. "No! It's true, I went into her room late that night to beg her to see reason. I suppose I was desperate." He was shaking. "And there she was. Dead."

"And while she lay there, dead, or possibly there was still life in her body and you might have saved her, you took her phone."

"No. It was too late. I swear it. I touched her and she was cold. So cold. Her phone was beside her, as though she'd just dropped it." He gulped. "I couldn't help her. There was nothing I could do." He was nearly in tears. "So, yes, I took the phone and as I told you, I threw it into the pond."

Jasper rose and took a step back. He kicked his chair as he did so and there was a hollow thud. "You liar. You murdered my wife!"

But I wasn't going to let Jasper get away with this little performance. I said, "But you also knew about the affair, didn't you, Jasper? But then this affair turned out to be quite convenient for you. If Malcolm Pritchard wasn't convicted of Tamsin's murder, you could always implicate Hugo."

"You should stick to arranging daisies," he said, snarling in my direction.

I took a breath. "But it was you who killed your wife."

Verity and Arabella both cried out in protest but I swallowed, determined to hold my own.

"It took me a while," I said, "but I managed to put all the pieces in place. I went to meet Gareth Callaghan. It was quite an interesting meeting. Your hedge fund was dumped by his firm over the weekend because it is, quite frankly, a shambles. It was only ever a question of time until the firm failed."

I glanced at Hugo. His mouth was hanging open. "What?" he cried. Clearly this was news to him. He'd had no idea.

I turned back to Jasper. "You and Tamsin were alike in some ways. You were both schemers. She wanted Hugo for his money and position. You were petrified she would leave you for Hugo and then Hugo might disband the hedge fund and he'd find out just how much money was missing. You were making wild bets. You got in deep, and the more you bet, the more you lost." I was following instinct and the energy coming off him. I'd had Alex talk me through how some of the more flamboyant and risky hedge fund managers had failed. I was certain Jasper had gone that way, too. Making bigger and bigger bets trying to erase his losses. But at some point, that hole would be too deep.

"Even your partner didn't know. You had to get money and fast. Killing Tamsin would mean you'd get five million in life insurance and some breathing time before your investors all pulled out. You hoped to turn things around. If Tamsin left you for Hugo, then all your disastrous investments would come to light." I paused, thinking back to my visit to his home in Chelsea. "And the cripplingly large mortgage," I said, taking a punt that they were mortgaged up to the hilt.

I studied Jasper's face as he turned even paler. I was obviously hitting a nerve. "You felt you had no choice. It was Tamsin's life or yours."

I looked around and saw that DI Rawlins was hovering in the doorway. She had brought Sergeant Evans with her. They stepped forward and walked towards the table. Jasper looked like he was about to make a run for it but I locked eyes with him and shook my head. "There's no escape from what you did, Jasper," I said.

"This is nonsense," he said, in an attempt to regain control. "I may have invested aggressively, it's what we do. But I wasn't even here when Tamsin was killed. I was in London. The police went over my car with a fine-tooth comb. I drove down here with my wife and drove back to London. I didn't return until this morning."

"You didn't drive down in your own car. You borrowed your wife's blue BMW."

When we'd seen the car in the driveway I'd remembered driving with Char, the car buff, on our way home late Saturday night. Char had mentioned the high-end vehicles we'd passed. I'd started paying attention then and seen the blue BMW. Char had even known which model it was. Not only was it the same model Tamsin drove, but what I'd thought was a scratch turned out to be parrot poop. While the police probably couldn't arrest Jasper Faringdon based on Norman's bad personal habits, there'd been rain during the night of Tamsin's murder and I was positive they would find traces of fresh mud in the tires consistent with this area. Tamsin definitely hadn't been driving her car that night. Her husband had.

"This is outrageous," Jasper claimed.

DI Rawlins said, "Mr. Faringdon, we would like you to come with us to the station to help us with our inquiries."

Jasper looked both furious and frightened. "Hugo," he ordered, "get hold of our solicitors. They'll know who to call."

But Hugo shook his head slowly. "Call them yourself. My solicitors will be busy dissolving our partnership."

Sergeant Evans left with Jasper.

Hugo turned to Verity who stood like a very angry statue. "Darling, let's go somewhere quiet and talk this thing through."

But Verity yanked at her enormous engagement ring and banged it onto the tabletop. "Hugo, I never want to see you again."

Arabella said, "Darling," and her daughter turned to her. "Right now, Mummy, I never want to see you, either. You knew, didn't you? You didn't even look a bit surprised."

"All I've ever wanted is what's best for you, darling," Arabella said.

Then Verity looked around the room as though not sure which way to turn. Gillian rose elegantly and came forward. "Why don't you come and stay at my house tonight? I have plenty of room. You can begin deciding your future tomorrow."

Verity looked more than grateful. "Thank you," she said.

I glanced at Lucas and I swear he fell more in love with Gillian at that moment. So did I, a little bit. Maybe Gillian hadn't always been the nicest woman in the world, but she was making up for that in a big way tonight.

After they left, DI Rawlins came up to our table. To my surprise, when Alex rose and offered to get her a chair, she agreed. She sat stiffly and grilled me with her detective's gaze.

"How did you, a local florist, discover some of these clues that our trained murder investigation team missed?" she asked.

"I'd spent time with all the people involved. I have good instincts about people." It was the best I could do. "I guess this means that Malcolm Pritchard can now be released?"

DI Rawlins nodded. "He already has been. It turns out that Malcolm Pritchard had been sleeping in his car the night of Tamsin Mortimer's murder. One of our police officers had seen a body slumped over the wheel and gone to check on him. It was in the police report. When we received the exact time of death from the mortuary, we knew that Pritchard couldn't have been the killer. He was with our officer, being told to move on." She smiled sourly. "So, you see, we don't always get it wrong."

I nodded, relieved that Malcolm Pritchard wasn't going to be punished for a crime he hadn't committed.

DI Rawlins continued, "When you suggested we look at Tamsin Mortimer's car earlier, it was a very good guess. It had recently been driven and there was fresh mud in the tires. Mr. Faringdon had used it to drive from London to the Cotswolds and back again unnoticed on Saturday night."

"The flashy blue BMW we saw driving back from your mom's house!" Char cried out.

I nodded.

DI Rawlins looked baffled. She said, "The BMW also had the same bird droppings on it that Mr. Faringdon's silver Ferrari did." She shrugged, obviously still puzzled by this detail. "And it was caught on CCTV once we knew to look for it. That was a good guess on your part."

I nodded. Sometimes Norman's mischievous streak really did have its uses.

Chapter Twenty-Three

T he next day, I was back at Bewitching Blooms, and it was business as usual. The drama of the previous night's arrest felt like a bad dream, but now I could rest easy knowing that the true culprit had been apprehended for Tamsin's murder.

I went to the chiller and retrieved the buckets of remaining flowers that should have been used on the course. There and then I decided to turn them into the lovely arrangements they had been intended for.

I ran my fingers over the petals of a few, admiring their delicate textures before getting to work. The rhythmic snip of the scissors was the only sound as I cut stems and placed them into vases, making sure each arrangement was just right. I said a spell of peace, closing my eyes as I imbued each bloom with hope. Whoever bought the new arrangements would change the course of these flowers' fates, giving them a new home where they could blossom as intended and bring true joy.

I worked quietly for an hour and was just tying the last

one when the door dinged and Verity walked in. She was alone.

"Hi," I said, stepping out from behind the counter to give her a hug. She looked pale and tired. Defeated, really, by all that had happened.

"I won't ask how you're doing," I said, "but I will put the kettle on instead."

She smiled gratefully and accepted a stool to sit down and rest for a moment.

I handed her a cup of camomile and lavender tea.

She thanked me and then said, "I don't know if my heart will ever be the same again."

I nodded. "It probably won't be the same, but it *will* heal. I can promise you that from personal experience."

She gave a weak smile. "I've decided to go on a trip alone. Take some time to think about things." She looked down at her hand minus the impressive diamond.

"I've lost everyone I held close, all at once. My best friend is dead, my fiancé was unfaithful, and my mother complicit. I don't know if I'll ever trust anyone again."

I reminded her that Gillian had stepped up and turned out to be a good friend. And I told her that I was always here if she wanted to talk.

I had the feeling Verity was much smarter than people gave her credit for. She didn't need the handsome but hapless Hugo hanging on her shirttails.

"I don't know if you knew this already, you seem to know everything before anyone else, but Jasper has admitted to the murder under questioning." Her eyes filled with tears. "He's been formally charged."

"Good," I said. "The right man was caught in the end."

"I still can't believe I've lost my best friend. Even if she was lying to me. I would have forgiven her, you know. For the affair. She's helped me see who Hugo really was. I've had a narrow escape there."

"And your mother?" I asked. "Will you eventually forgive her?"

She shrugged. "I'm pretty angry with her. I can't believe she knew about the affair and didn't tell me. That's why I'm taking this trip. To get away from everyone and find myself again."

"It sounds like a good idea," I agreed. "Go somewhere hot, where the flowers and the cocktails are tropical."

Verity laughed weakly. "And I thought a weekend arranging roses would be a good thing."

"Maybe knowing the truth was a good thing in the end." I bent down and gave her one of the new bouquets I'd made from the leftover flowers. I hoped it would give her optimism for her new life ahead, one begun in independence and truth.

She thanked me for the tea and the flowers and the kind words and then said she had to leave to head back to London.

"Alone?"

She shook her head. "Lucas Chen is driving me. He has to get back to the city. When I return from my travels, Gillian has invited me to stay for as long as I like. I may just do that."

"I hope so. I look forward to seeing you again."

We embraced.

As she was leaving, Alex walked in. I felt my heart warm when our gazes connected.

"I thought you could do with a date this evening," he said. "Somewhere cozy, with expensive red wine, where we can put this past weekend to rest."

"Sounds perfect," I said. "I'll be finished up here soon. We can head out together."

He smiled and took the seat which Verity had just vacated. "You know," he said, as I began to close up the till, "it feels a bit unfair that the police are taking credit for your investigative skills. Without you, they would have never arrested Jasper."

"All that matters is that they got the right man in the end. All I want is to live in Willow Waters and have a quiet life arranging flowers." I reached into a bucket, plucked out a bright red carnation, and placed it in his buttonhole.

He smiled down at me. "Why do I think that's unlikely?"

Thanks for reading *Game of Thorns*. I hope you'll consider leaving a review, it really helps.

While you're waiting for the next *Village Flower Shop* adventure, have you tried my *The Great Witches Baking Show* series yet? Here's a peek from book 1.

The Great Witches Baking Show, Prologue

ELSPETH PEACH COULD NOT HAVE CONJURED A MORE beautiful day. Broomewode Hall glowed in the spring sunshine. The golden Cotswolds stone manor house was a Georgian masterpiece, and its symmetrical windows winked at her as though it knew her secrets and promised to keep them. Green lawns stretched their arms wide, and an ornamental lake seemed to welcome the swans floating serene and elegant on its surface.

But if she shifted her gaze just an inch to the left, the sense of peace and tranquility broke into a million pieces. Trucks and trailers had invaded the grounds, large tents were already in place, and she could see electricians and carpenters and painters at work on the twelve cooking stations. As the star judge of the wildly popular TV series *The Great British Baking Contest,* Elspeth Peach liked to cast her discerning eye over the setup to make sure that everything was perfect.

When the reality show became a hit, Elspeth Peach had been rocketed to a household name. She'd have been just as happy to be left alone in relative obscurity, writing cookbooks and devising new recipes. When she'd first agreed to judge amateur bakers, she'd imagined a tiny production watched only by serious foodies, and with a limited run. Had she known the show would become an international success, she never would have agreed to become so public a figure. Because Elspeth Peach had an important secret to keep. She was an excellent baker, but she was an even better witch.

Elspeth had made a foolish mistake. Baking made her happy, and she wanted to spread some of that joy to others. But she never envisaged how popular the series would become or how closely she'd be scrutinized by The British Witches Council, the governing body of witches in the UK. The council wielded great power, and any witch who didn't follow the rules was punished.

When she'd been unknown, she'd been able to fudge the borders of rule-following a bit. She always obeyed the main tenet of a white witch—do no harm. However, she wasn't so good at the dictates about not interfering with mortals without good reason. Now, she knew she was being watched very carefully, and she'd have to be vigilant. Still, as nervous as she was about her own position, she was more worried about her brand-new co-host.

Jonathon Pine was another famous British baker. His cookbooks rivaled hers in popularity and sales, so it shouldn't have been a surprise that he'd been chosen as her co-judge. Except that Jonathon was also a witch.

She'd argued passionately against the council's decision to have him as her co-judge, but it was no good. She was stuck with him. And that put the only cloud in the blue sky of this lovely day.

To her surprise, she saw Jonathon approaching her. She'd imagined he'd be the type to turn up a minute before cameras began rolling. He was an attractive man of about fifty with sparkling blue eyes and thick, dark hair. However, at this moment he looked sheepish, more like a sulky boy than a baking celebrity. Her innate empathy led her to get right to the issue that was obviously bothering him, and since she was at least twenty years his senior, she said in a motherly tone, "Has somebody been a naughty witch?"

He met her gaze then. "You know I have. I'm sorry, Elspeth. The council says I have to do this show." He poked at a stone with the toe of his signature cowboy boot—one of his affectations, along with the blue shirts he always wore to bring out the color of his admittedly very pretty eyes.

"But how are you going to manage it?"

"I'm hoping you'll help me."

She shook her head at him. "Five best-selling books and a

consultant to how many bakeries and restaurants? What were you thinking?"

He jutted out his bottom lip. "It started as a bit of a lark, but things got out of control. I became addicted to the fame."

"But you know we're not allowed to use our magic for personal gain."

He'd dug out the stone now with the toe of his boot, and his attention dropped to the divot he'd made in the lawn. "I know, I know. It all started innocently enough. This woman I met said no man can bake a proper scone. Well, I decided to show her that wasn't true by baking her the best scone she'd ever tasted. All right, I used a spell, since I couldn't bake a scone or anything else, for that matter. But it was a matter of principle. And then one thing led to another."

"Tell me the truth, Jonathon. Can you bake at all? Without using magic, I mean."

A worm crawled lazily across the exposed dirt, and he followed its path. She found herself watching the slow, curling brown body too, hoping. Finally, he admitted, "I can't boil water."

She could see that the council had come up with the perfect punishment for him by making the man who couldn't bake a celebrity judge. He was going to be publicly humiliated. But, unfortunately, so was she.

He groaned. "If only I'd said no to that first book deal. That's when the real trouble started."

Privately, she thought it was when he magicked a scone into being. It was too easy to become addicted to praise and far too easy to slip into inappropriate uses of magic. One bad move could snowball into catastrophe. And now look where they were.

When he raised his blue eyes to meet hers, he looked quite desperate. "The council told me I had to learn how to bake and come and do this show without using any magic at all." He sighed. "Or else."

"Or else?" Her eyes squinted as though the sun were blinding her, but really she dreaded the answer.

He lowered his voice. "Banishment."

She took a sharp breath. "As bad as that?"

He nodded. "And you're not entirely innocent either, you know. They told me you've been handing out your magic like it's warm milk and cuddles. You've got to stop, Elspeth, or it's banishment for you, too."

She swallowed. Her heart pounded. She couldn't believe the council had sent her a message via Jonathon rather than calling her in themselves. She'd never used her magic for personal gain, as Jonathon had. She simply couldn't bear to see these poor, helpless amateur bakers blunder when she could help. They were so sweet and eager. She became attached to them all. So sometimes she turned on an oven if a baker forgot or saved the biscuits from burning, the custard from curdling. She'd thought no one had noticed.

However, she had steel in her as well as warm milk, and she spoke quite sternly to her new co-host. "Then we must make absolutely certain that nothing goes wrong this season. You will practice every recipe before the show. Learn what makes a good crumpet, loaf of bread and Victoria sponge. You will study harder than you ever have in your life, Jonathon. I will help you where I can, but I won't go down with you."

He leveled her with an equally steely gaze. "All right. And

you won't interfere. If some show contestant forgets to turn their oven on, you don't make it happen by magic."

Oh dear. So they *did* know all about her little intervention in Season Two.

"And if somebody's caramelized sugar starts to burn, you do not save it."

Oh dear. And that.

"Fine. I will let them flail and fail, poor dears."

"And I'll learn enough to get by. We'll manage, Elspeth."

The word banishment floated in the air between them like the soft breeze.

"We'll have to."

Read the rest of *The Great Witches Baking Show* or sign up for my newsletter at NancyWarrenAuthor.com to hear about all of my new releases.

A Note from Nancy

Dear Reader,

Thank you for reading *Game of Thorns*. I hope you'll consider leaving a review and please tell your friends who like flowers and paranormal cozy mysteries. Review on my website, Amazon, Goodreads or BookBub.

I'm always grateful for the help and support of friends and readers. *Game of Thorns* is a title dreamed up by the brilliant Linda J. Hall. Linda loves a good pun and my life would be infinitely poorer without her in it. Thanks, Linda. I think you'll see a few more of your titles coming up in this series. Thanks to all my beta readers who catch my mistakes before the books are published.

Join my newsletter for a free prequel, *Tangles and Treason*, the exciting tale of how the gorgeous Rafe Crosyer, from *The Vampire Knitting Club* series, was turned into a vampire.

I hope to see you in my private Facebook Group. It's a lot of fun. www.facebook.com/groups/NancyWarrenKnitwits

Until next time,
Happy Reading,

Nancy

Also by Nancy Warren

The best way to keep up with new releases, plus enjoy bonus content and prizes is to join Nancy's newsletter at NancyWarrenAuthor.com or join her in her private Facebook group Nancy Warren's Knitwits.

Village Flower Shop: Paranormal Cozy Mystery

In a picture-perfect Cotswold village, flowers, witches, and murder make quite the bouquet for flower shop owner Peony Bellefleur.

Peony Dreadful - Book 1

Karma Camellia - Book 2

Highway to Hellebore - Book 3

Luck of the Iris - Book 4

Game of Thorns - Book 5

Vampire Knitting Club: Paranormal Cozy Mystery

Lucy Swift inherits an Oxford knitting shop and the late-night knitting club of vampires who live downstairs.

Tangles and Treason - A free ebook for newsletter subscribers. A paperback version is available for sale. NancyWarrenAuthor.com

The Vampire Knitting Club - Book 1

Stitches and Witches - Book 2

Crochet and Cauldrons - Book 3

Stockings and Spells - Book 4

Purls and Potions - Book 5

Fair Isle and Fortunes - Book 6

Lace and Lies - Book 7

Bobbles and Broomsticks - Book 8

Popcorn and Poltergeists - Book 9

Garters and Gargoyles - Book 10

Diamonds and Daggers - Book 11

Herringbones and Hexes - Book 12

Ribbing and Runes - Book 13

Mosaics and Magic - Book 14

Cables and Conjurers - Book 15

Cat's Paws and Curses - A Holiday Whodunnit

Vampire Knitting Club Mega Paperback Series Bundle

Vampire Knitting Club Boxed Set: Books 1-3

Vampire Knitting Club Boxed Set: Books 4-6

Vampire Knitting Club Boxed Set: Books 7-9

Vampire Knitting Club Boxed Set: Books 10-12

Vampire Knitting Club: Cornwall: Paranormal Cozy Mystery

Boston-bred witch Jennifer Cunningham agrees to run a knitting and yarn shop in a fishing village in Cornwall, England—with characters from the Oxford-set *Vampire Knitting Club* series.

The Vampire Knitting Club: Cornwall - Book 1

Scallops and Sorcerers - Book 2

Vampire Book Club: Paranormal Women's Fiction Cozy Mystery

Seattle witch Quinn Callahan's midlife crisis is interrupted when she gets sent to Ballydehag, Ireland, to run an unusual bookshop.

Crossing the Lines - Prequel

The Vampire Book Club - Book 1

Chapter and Curse - Book 2

A Spelling Mistake - Book 3

A Poisonous Review - Book 4

In Want of a Knife - Book 5

Vampire Book Club Boxed Set: Books 1-3

Great Witches Baking Show: Paranormal Culinary Cozy Mystery

Poppy Wilkinson, an American with English roots, joins a reality show to win the crown of Britain's Best Baker—and to get inside Broomewode Hall to uncover the secrets of her past.

The Great Witches Baking Show - Book 1

Baker's Coven - Book 2

A Rolling Scone - Book 3

A Bundt Instrument - Book 4

Blood, Sweat and Tiers - Book 5

Crumbs and Misdemeanors - Book 6

A Cream of Passion - Book 7

Cakes and Pains - Book 8

Whisk and Reward - Book 9

Gingerdead House - A Holiday Whodunnit

The Great Witches Baking Show Boxed Set: Books 1-3

The Great Witches Baking Show Boxed Set: Books 4-6 (includes bonus novella)

The Great Witches Baking Show Boxed Set: Books 7-9

Toni Diamond Mysteries

Toni Diamond is a successful saleswoman for Lady Bianca Cosmetics in this series of humorous cozy mysteries.

Frosted Shadow - Book 1

Ultimate Concealer - Book 2

Midnight Shimmer - Book 3

A Diamond Choker For Christmas - A Holiday Whodunnit

Toni Diamond Mysteries Boxed Set: Books 1-4

Abigail Dixon: 1920s Cozy Historical Mystery

In 1920s Paris everything is très chic, except murder.

Murder at the Paris Fashion House - Book 1

Death at Darrington Manor - Book 2

The Almost Wives Club: Contemporary Romantic Comedy

An enchanted wedding dress is a matchmaker in this series of romantic comedies where five runaway brides find out who the best men really are.

The Almost Wives Club: Kate - Book 1

Secondhand Bride - Book 2

Bridesmaid for Hire - Book 3

The Wedding Flight - Book 4

If the Dress Fits - Book 5

The Almost Wives Club Boxed Set: Books 1-5

Take a Chance: Contemporary Romance

Meet the Chance family, a cobbled together family of eleven kids who are all grown up and finding their ways in life and love.

Chance Encounter - Prequel

Kiss a Girl in the Rain - Book 1

Iris in Bloom - Book 2

Blueprint for a Kiss - Book 3

Every Rose - Book 4

Love to Go - Book 5

The Sheriff's Sweet Surrender - Book 6

The Daisy Game - Book 7

Take a Chance Boxed Set: Prequel and Books 1-3

For a complete list of books, check out Nancy's website at NancyWarrenAuthor.com

About the Author

Nancy Warren is the USA Today Bestselling author of more than 100 novels. She's originally from Vancouver, Canada, though she tends to wander and has lived in England, Italy, and California at various times. While living in Oxford she dreamed up The Vampire Knitting Club. Favorite moments include being the answer to a crossword puzzle clue in Canada's National Post newspaper, being featured on the front page of the New York Times when her book *Speed Dating* launched Harlequin's NASCAR series, and being nominated three times for Romance Writers of America's RITA award. She has an MA in Creative Writing from Bath Spa University. She's an avid hiker, loves chocolate, and most of all, loves to hear from readers!

The best way to stay in touch is to sign up for Nancy's newsletter at NancyWarrenAuthor.com or www.facebook.com/groups/NancyWarrenKnitwits

To learn more about Nancy and her books
NancyWarrenAuthor.com

facebook.com/AuthorNancyWarren

x.com/nancywarren1

instagram.com/nancywarrenauthor

amazon.com/Nancy-Warren/e/B001H6NM5Q

goodreads.com/nancywarren

bookbub.com/authors/nancy-warren